Up Where I Used to Live

ILLINOIS SHORT FICTION

Up Where I Used to Live

Stories by
Max Schott

UNIVERSITY OF ILLINOIS PRESS

Urbana   Chicago   London

Manufactured in the United States of America

This project is supported by a grant from the National Endowment for the Arts in Washington, D.C., a Federal agency.

"Sterling's Calf," *Spectrum,* Spring, 1971
"Early Winter," *Massachusetts Review,* vol. 4, no. 1, 1978
"The Old Flame" (original title: "Murphy Jones: Pearblossom, California"), *Ascent,* vol. 2, no. 2, 1977; *Best American Short Stories of 1978* (Doubleday)
"The Horsebreaker," *Ascent,* vol. 2, no. 3, 1977
"The Drowning," *Ascent,* vol. 3, no. 3, 1978

Library of Congress Cataloging in Publication Data

Schott, Max, 1935-
  Up where I used to live.

  (Illinois short fiction)
  CONTENTS: Up where I used to live.—Sterling's calf.—Early winter. [etc.]
  I. Title.
PZ4.S374Up [PS3569.C5263]   813'.5'4   78-11619
ISBN 0-252-00719-0
ISBN 0-252-00720-4 pbk.

For
Elaine Schott and Bob Hymer

Contents

Up Where I Used to Live

For God knows what reasons, I never liked to hunt. Tis is, morally, a touchy subject. Most people who don't like to hunt affect moral scruples about it. Whether they really don't like to hunt because of these moral scruples will always be impossible to say—but pardon me if I suspect them, especially if they eat a hamburger now and then. If they eat no hamburgers, I suppose I have to grant them their moral scruples—I immediately suspect them of other things, but let that go. Anyway, in my own case: I didn't like to hunt, I ate my hamburgers (and venison too, if anyone would give it to me), and considered myself to have moral scruples. I was rather cagey about these though, and without really fooling anyone else I managed to deceive myself. (And if in this I'm different from anyone else, I've yet to notice it.)

My parents were big-city liberals, my father an unpretentious, modest man, even apologetic (and I have my quarrel with that, too, but let it pass). If liberalism is a sin, I hold him responsible for introducing me to it, though I never observed in him the infamous holier-than-thou taint of the practicing liberal; I'm afraid I found that for myself.

Later I held this (holier-than-thou) attitude the more strongly, I think, because of the life I'd elected to lead. I was a horse trainer and lived out in the country, where my neighbors were farmers.

These farmer neighbors considered me a sort of outlander—though they couldn't have been more civil. They forgave me the fact that I wasn't born there, that I slept till eight on Sundays (even in the summertime when it had been light for hours), that I could sometimes be seen washing the dishes myself, that I borrowed more equipment than I lent, and many other trivial peculiarities; and I forgave them their antique political opinions, their steady routines, their ability to put aside money, their affection for machines, their refusal to let my little children undress their little children, and so on. But one must pronounce the word "forgave" with a slight ironic emphasis. On both sides, there was always the sense of something being withheld. What was withheld was, I say, for the most part bad, and so it was just as well; but still, one of the effects was that we had closed countenances. And reason about it as you might, the closed countenance, though nearly universal, and though certainly more appealing than the affectation of an open countenance, is still not pleasing.

It was a good country for hunting. To shoot a goose or duck, if you lived in my neighborhood, you only had to step out the door. And about a mile to the east was a mountain, where you could find plenty of mule deer. This mountain was an ugly, barren affair and looked like a big molehill. It blocked the sunrise, and so I had a personal grudge against it. You'd think a person would get used to such things, but I never did. But the other side, if you rode up over the top, was different—forested and broad. Up there, oh maybe ten miles back, was where my farmer neighbors kept a hunting camp. Every fall they'd go up there for a week or more.

Hunting aside, country people are different in their attitude toward their fellow creatures—from city people I mean. Or at least they express themselves differently. They are little given, for example, to expressing generalized sentiments about animals. For the sake of the argument, you can consider me a country person in this respect. Take the statement "I love horses." I've no idea what to make of it. Country people rarely say such things, and tend to frown stupidly when they hear them. I saw a picture-puzzle of a horse once, and had no idea what it was! Such is the penalty of knowing too much. And my confusion is exemplary: these people, whose lives and livelihoods are all tangled up with animals, have their sentiments all in a tangle too. City people, on the other hand, have here the clearness of an empty brain. They used to say to me, in all innocence: "So you like horses, do you?" What could I say? One time I'd say, "Yes, I like them a lot." Another time I'd say, "No, I hate most of them, actually." A third time I'd say that in general I was indifferent to them, though some I respected. And sometimes again I'd say I liked them best when they misbehaved, for then I could hit them between the ears with my fist (humane fellow that I am, I never used to hit them if they didn't misbehave and then only with my fist, which I often bruised). Anyway, whatever I said, I would later be bothered and feel I'd lied, though usually I'd answered, as far as I knew, sincerely. After all, you don't always feel the same after dinner as before, if you know what I mean.

If you live around animals you get, like a doctor, used to being a little bloody-handed. Take the way porcupines were thought of, for example. There was a bounty on them of fifty cents apiece. This was paid, very reasonably, on receipt of a nose (for who wants to carry whole dead porcupines around, and what would be the point of it?). The result of this was that people—especially up on the reservation north of town, where there was a thriving porcupine-killing business—people talked not about the living animal, the porcupine, but about porcupine noses, or just "noses." Many people, mostly young Indians, drove around at night hoping to pay for their gas (which in any case they often stole) by catching porcupines in the headlights, killing them, and cutting off their noses—as if pop bottles had legs. So by "bloody-handed" I don't mean anything nasty and metaphorical. If it sounds unpleasant, that's because really who does want to have blood on their hands?

From an early age I took up with animals, and it was this that led me, gradually and almost without my noticing, to a rural existence. As a kid I was very squeamish—couldn't bear the sight of blood. And I could never have anticipated or imagined then the things I would have to get used to just because I happened to like messing around with animals.

I remember what a time I had learning to give simple injections, and the suffering I caused any number of nags by my clumsiness bred of fear, and the many needles I broke and bent trying in my clumsy, chicken-hearted way to shove them through cows' hides. The first time I was in a branding corral, too, I became so woozy and pale that when I came in to lunch the women noticed. As I got older I got used to syringes, castrating knives, festering wounds, etc., but I kept a bit of the old feeling.

Now squeamishness is an ugly, unwholesome trait, and when I was little, and when I was a teen-ager too, I was full of self-disgust at the very idea of this feeling in myself. So I made efforts. Let me say to my own credit that, for example, when I was twenty I used to kill and butcher my own beef. But that was about my last stand. As I got older I gradually acquired, for no reason I can think of, a much higher opinion of myself. And this very same squeamishness that I had once done battle against I began imperceptibly to use as evidence for my own tenderheartedness and humaneness—for my *sensitivity*. Most, if not all men—and certainly my conservative hunting farmer neighbors—were more barbaric and coldblooded than I. Such was my unspoken conviction.

2

So my neighbors went hunting every fall.

During the winter they slogged through the mud and snow, forking out to their herds of cattle the hay which they spent the summer irrigating, mowing, raking, turning, baling, hauling.

Cows eat every day, a fact no one will question but which, living in such a place, you keep getting reminded of. No holiday for the cow's belly or any of its stomachs and none for the hay-forking farmer. But actually he gets up and feeds his cows on Christmas morning as naturally as most of us pick our noses, and with no more sense of oppression. Still, a holiday would be pleasant. They worked like the devil (day and night) in the summer, were tied to the persistent belly of the cow in the winter, and there was no spring (winter, about a month after you'd lost hope, one day turned to summer and that was that).

But fall was the glorious season. The weather was good, the crops were in, nothing grew (since it froze every night), the irrigation water was shut off at the source (I would soon be galloping my horses up and down the empty ditches and canals), and the cows were feeding themselves in the stubble fields. And so my neighbors—not having had enough of dirt, weather, and long hours—went hunting. As people do, they began thinking of it long ahead—in fact they talked about these trips the whole year long, both the ones coming and the ones that had been. But I mean here that by the middle of summer, when they'd been working like mad for a couple of months and still had plenty of the same ahead of them and when everything was still growing like crazy, my neighbors already had an eye cocked toward the mountain and were studying with more than ordinary interest the deer that came down and crossed the road into the fields in the evenings.

And so one day early in August, my neighbor Glenn brought over his jenny to see if I could trim her feet for him. They used this donkey as a pack animal to carry their buck from wherever he might be lying with his throat cut out to where they could get at him with a pickup. And this was the only thing they used her for; the whole rest of the year she just ran in the pasture with the cows. This little foot-trimming session turned into a sort of mild holiday gathering itself. The farmers, in other words, took a couple of hours off and stood around together to watch, as if something important was going on. Supposedly they came over to help and to see if she might kick my teeth in: they'd had some trouble with her before; and from the looks of her hooves, which were long and turned up in front like an old goat's, they hadn't wrastled among themselves with farmerly eagerness over the job of trimming her. But I was in danger of getting my teeth kicked in every day, and usually no one bothered to watch.

The burro was in a tractable mood. (In the past they'd probably just held her feet up too high). And yet, when it became apparent she wasn't going to put up a fuss, not a one of them left to go back to work.

Not everyone who went to the camp was there, only three: Herman
Wise (a Jew, but as far as I could see this meant nothing either to
him or the others); Glenn Yarnell, the villain or, if you prefer, the
hero of the story; and a third man who was married to Glenn's sister
and who I'll just call the brother-in-law, since that's mostly how the
poor fellow was thought of.

Our places all adjoined each other, two on each side of the county
road. About twenty years before, all of our farms still belonged to
old Sam Yarnell, Glenn's father. When he died the property was di-
vided up among his four children; since then, two of them had sold
out, one to me and one to Herman. But Herman wasn't a newcomer;
he'd had a bigger farm just a few miles away. Now he was getting on
in years, had socked a little money away, and kept most of his new
place in pasture, which took the least work to care for. Although he
did enough to satisfy most people, he was a kind of putterer compared to what he'd been once, or compared to Glenn or even to the
brother-in-law. He was a widower with white hair and had a sort of
naturally elegant bearing, though he was shy. He had the reputa-
tion, Herman did, of being a "fine old man," and I never saw or
heard of anything to indicate he wasn't, but I supposed he could
spatter a deer's brains as well as the next person.

The brother-in-law was a goodhearted or—if such a description is
out of place here—a hearty, sort of impulsive person, who was in the
awkward position of having married a girl with a little property when
he himself had nothing. To make it worse, she'd got the worst of old
man Yarnell's farmland, and the poor guy could never quite make
ends meet. I don't remember how many acres he had, but the best of
it was a sidehill that sloped off the foot of the mountain, and the
worst of it was a big strip of flat alkali land which, no matter how
much he flushed water through it and in spite of all the thousands of
pickup loads of organic matter of various kinds he and his kids
dumped there and plowed into the ground, nothing worth mention-
ing would grow on—nothing but salt grass. Twice that I know of, he
had to go to town and work. This likeable person seemed to breathe
failure. Once he brought me two horses to train for his kids. He'd
raised them himself. Neither of them was even worth feeding, as he

must have known, and for the price of the training he could have bought a couple of decent ones already trained. That is to say, he was sentimental.

Like Herman (who, remember, was old and a widower), the brother-in-law was a guy you could feel for: a little pitiable; not too, just enough.

Glenn was another story. Someone, for all I know, may have liked him, but pity him you couldn't. He was a prospering, hardworking, healthy, self-confident man, very easy—if you are at all like me—to envy. Or rather, you *could* pity him, with a kind of effort of will, and I did, but it never came out quite right; he didn't seem to really *receive* the feeling, even in my imagination, and (as you may know) this is disconcerting.

He himself knew he had it made. I could tell this just from the way his head sat on his shoulders, or nearly on his shoulders—he had one of those thick necks farmers are so well known for; red, too, at least during August. A regular peasant, and since he had no intention or likelihood of being hanged for anything, there's no reason to believe that this head of his wasn't every bit as solidly established as it appeared to be to me. He thought he had it made, though being a superstitious and modest man he would certainly never have said so. (There is the possibility, of course, that I misrepresent his deeper feelings—but I consider this mere logical quibbling.)

And he did have it made. His place was bought and paid for, and death alone would take him away from it. In his lifetime he'd lived in three houses—all on this same road and each better than the one before. He liked doing what he did, was good at it, and had never conceived of doing anything else. When he drove from his house to the foot of the mountain and crossed the railroad track, as he did more than once every day, he passed a sign with his name on it—*Yarnell*—erected by the Northern Pacific to identify the siding. I imagine he wasn't often moved to feel that "there but for the grace of God go I." "There by the grace of God goes someone else" would be closer to it.

Such complacent beings—apparently unassailable by civilized methods—annoy the daylights out of their betters—a phenomenon

I've noticed taking place in more brains than just my own. Only God can settle the hash of these fellows, that's the problem, and He'll have to wait until they're on their deathbeds. *Then* they'll be made to toss and turn and look for the light at the end of the bag—or so one hopes. And where will I be then?

He was a good guy. Everyone said so, and when you talked to him, there was nothing to take exception to; he'd never done anyone any harm, he wasn't ungenerous; so there was no way to get around him, and as I say, he lived right across the road.

3

Every situation is (if you like simplicity) intolerably complicated. Here, for instance, this rustic scene. Without a spreading chestnut, true; yet we're proceeding romantically enough. I'm standing bent double like a frog right out in the hot sun, holding the pencil-like leg of a burro between my knees and rasping away, pausing to sight a line down her hoof once in a while, in order to give the impression that I'm concerned to do a good job. Herman, the brother-in-law, and Glenn repose in farmerly attitudes, watching. Tree or no, we were the kind of group people stop to take pictures of.

The brother-in-law was hunkering on his heels, hat pushed back revealing the white of his forehead, probably in imitation of some ad or movie he'd seen.

Herman, because he was shy, dignified, and a widower, stood squarely on his feet, holding the lead rope of the burro close to her jaw; he watched both me and her (though she was half asleep) with faithful attention, prepared, I suppose, to save my life.

Glenn, who was rather fat (he may have worked, but he also ate), sat on a special contraption I'd built out of railroad ties. How conscious he was of what he was sitting on, I don't know. But this must be explained too. You see how complicated everything is, even among rustics!

All the while, the sweat was running. Much of it dripped secretly under my clothes, out of sight, and I felt the loss and the pity of the loss. But gradually the blessed stuff soaked through the back of my shirt, where they couldn't help but see it, and began to fall drop by drop from the end of my nose. I didn't begrudge them this sweat; far from it—provided they saw it. I wanted them to see how freely I gave. No doubt each drop made them regret a little more that they'd brought over the burro, since she seemed to be so gentle now and since I seemed to sweat with such facility—but that was their problem. I was greedily adding up—drop by drop—future favors due; and if you find that incompatible with generosity—well, I don't know what to say.

The contraption Glenn was sitting on was a sort of stocks. When a mare was ready to be bred, I'd put her in there, so that the stallion could get a better shot at her. This servicing, as it's called by animal lovers, was a service which, while some mares liked it to a degree almost embarrassing, some didn't appreciate, and it was for those cantankerous ones that I'd built the stocks. But it didn't work for them, and caused more trouble and injury than it prevented. For the good, gentle, healthy, passionate, and willing ones, though, it had turned out to be useful. It kept them still. They—sweet things, who wanted nothing more than to receive the full surge and thrust of their heart's desire—found it hard to do so without help. It's almost impossible to stand still with a stallion on your back, no matter how much you may want to; and though she may have wished, if anything, to go backward, she was pushed forward. But not with my stocks.

I could help, even without it, by standing in front of the mare, braced against her chest, and I had often done this; but the trouble is I was needed behind, too, to hold her tail to the side and guide the penis with my hand—often neither the stallion nor the mare, with the best will in the world, was as proficient as they might have wished.

I did this work (which was duller than it sounds, let me tell you) by myself, but very often there was an audience of silent children, among whom, for a while, were Glenn's two little girls. But long before the day of the jenny-trimming (in fact as soon as Glenn found out about it), he'd disallowed them to watch any more, farm girls or not. I never saw kids, his and the others too, watch anything with more attention, day after day. I told them not to move or talk if they were going to hang around, and orders were never more faithfully obeyed. Any grade-school teacher would have envied me. If you ever want your kids kept quiet and out of trouble, horse-breeding is much to be recommended. Unluckily, if you live in California there are laws against the spectacle, and it must be done behind solid walls of a specified height which I've forgotten, but high enough so you'd be lucky to even see his ears.

This is where Glenn, then, was sitting. A whole essay could be written on these unrecorded passions. One young stallion I used to let the mares kick if they felt like it; he got to be a terrific dodger and eventually developed such remarkable intuitions that he rarely even had to dodge. Within a couple of years he turned himself gradually into a lover. At his prime, if she was cold and unfriendly, for example, he would show no interest and that was that. But if she was in heat and only *thought* herself unfriendly, he would do what was right. He always did, the stupid beast, and how he could tell I've no idea. He might grab her by the neck with his teeth or turn and kick her a time or two—which, when he chose to do it, changed her mood for the better (a dangerous proceeding from which I mean no analogical conclusions to be drawn at all—if he hadn't been such a good dodger his legs would have been broken for him many times over).

On the other hand, he might divine that, although she was winking and pissing and squatting—showing, to my eye, all the signs—she was simply not ready, and then he'd refuse to have anything to do with her till the next day. He wouldn't mount her if she weren't ready to mount, whether this meant getting her ready himself or just waiting. When she was ready, he might enter with little ado with no help from anyone and breed her perfunctorily—many of them he just didn't seem to be wild about. But there were those mares he plainly liked—a lot of them, too, maybe half. These he would lick from head to tail, sometimes with an erection and sometimes not. He'd lick them all over, from their feet up and their ears back, in spite of the fact that they'd long been won over (as he well knew, if I may dare so assert). Most especially he licked the front legs, shoulders, neck, and withers, but always on the left side only, for some reason—maybe a habit I'd got him into in the old days before I gave him free rein.

There was one mare he would never court or breed at all—one out of hundreds, though the other stallions seemed to like her well enough and she wasn't uglier or more objectionable than the rest as far as I could see. But they say everyone is crazy in his own way. . . .

4

"How long is it before you're going to use her?" I asked, knowing the answer as well as they did.

"Maybe six weeks, wouldn't you say, Herman?" Glenn said.

"Sure no sooner than that, unless you want to poach one."

"You ever had to shoe her?" (I was just trimming her feet remember.)

"Never have. But her feet got a little sore running around up over those mountain rocks last year," Glenn said. "First time."

"That's right, she did get sore didn't she," said the brother-in-law; "I'd forgot about that. Getting a little age on her I suppose, and packing around that field full of grass she's eaten—got quite a belly on her for such a little old thing."

"Pity you can't turn her out on the mountain there herself for a month or two before the season," I said. "She'd have the prettiest little feet you can imagine and keep herself legged up, too. You ever see the foot on a wild burro?—just like a chunk of obsidian."

"That's so," Glenn said; "be the best thing in the world for her, but she's taken up with the cows, you know; thinks she's a cow; and you know how the kids and wife would squeal if I kicked her out in those rocks. I don't doubt it would be a good thing." He said this out of politeness—obviously he doubted it would be a good thing. At the word "squeal," or just after it, he had put his hands behind him and pushed himself up, as if casually, off my stocks. Of course it could have been a coincidence, but I thought to myself and felt like saying aloud, "They didn't squeal, Glenn. The mare squealed a little, but your girls never moved a muscle." "Thinks she's a cow, does she?" I said politely.

"There's an old boy down in Etna I used to sell a tractor to once in a while," said the brother-in-law—one of his attempts to keep afloat had been as a tractor salesman—"had a wild jabalina pig used to run with the cows: darndest thing you ever saw; stuck with one bunch and you couldn't even run those cattle through a chute without him being under their feet, let alone separate him out at a gate."

"Boar, was it?" Herman said.

"Little gelding," the brother-in-law said. "They caught him when he was just a little thing and castrated him, thinking to fatten him for Easter. But the kids made such a pet of him they finally decided to turn him loose again, but the little bugger wouldn't go. I watched him fight a bull one day: funniest thing, back off and grunt and paw the ground and run right at each other; bull couldn't get his head low enough and Easter couldn't get his up off the ground—zip, right under the bull's belly and then they'd turn around, eyeball each other, grunt and paw the ground and go again." (It was in this unenlightened fashion that we blabbered on.)

I rested, leaning on the burro's back between feet; the longer a job takes the bigger it seems—nor was I used to bending over so far.

When I got done they thanked me again. And I made a joke about how they'd better wait till the next day and see if she was lame before feeling too grateful. I should have waited until the next day to make my joke, or at least until they led her off. She was lame. I had to make another joke. We all joked. Privately, I figured she was just surprised to have lost so much foot, but there's no use trying to explain such things to the owner. In a day or two, she'd be all right, but no matter—such impressions are indelible. Well, damn her and them too, I thought to myself. They'd remember the way she walked off and forget all about the sweat—all that sweat! But we parted friendly, as people do.

I don't remember exactly, but it was right around that same time that the roan mare turned up sick. I noticed her in the afternoon, when I was out riding some clobber-headed colt through a field: she was standing off away from the other horses, holding her head askew like a person with a crick in their neck. I thought that was what she had herself, and since she was as wild as the day she was born I had no intention of inspecting her at very close quarters. But when I checked her again in the evening, in the duller light I couldn't help but notice that her eye was feverish—all surface and a glittery surface at that, and she hadn't moved and must not have eaten. So I called the vet.

He came out before dark—meanwhile I'd run her into a corral—and first off when he looked at her he said she had sleeping sickness. I told him that when I'd vaccinated the horses in the spring I'd let her go, her and a couple of others, because they were too wild to risk messing with unless you absolutely had to.

We roped her and pulled her down and he gave her a big shot of something, saying at the same time that it probably wouldn't do any good, which it didn't.

One of those wild old mares—a different one—kicked me all the way across the corral one day; it was a small corral, about twenty-five feet, but still that's pretty impressive. If she hadn't happened to catch me right on the fat part of my leg, I'd probably be seeking God from a prone position right now (if at all) instead of from this straight-backed easy chair.

I rather liked the mare that kicked me. "Skinny," we called her. At the moment she kicked me I had her helplessly secured, according to all sensible notions: one hind leg tied up under her belly with a big fat rope, so that she had to keep the other leg on the ground or else flounder and fall down. (She had a stallion bite on her hip, and that's what I was doctoring.) In this position, so I used to think, a horse can't kick. I had years of experience to verify it, and you can try it yourself: get down on all fours, lift one leg, and see how much you can then do with the other one. But she rocked forward on her front toes and kicked me never the less far for all my blessed experience.

The other mare, the roan, I'd never much cared for. She had a good colt every year, but she herself left me cold—I couldn't really say why. Still, it irritated me that she was sick—apparently unto death—and it wasn't just the money, either. The sight of any sick animal always used to irritate me.

We—the vet and I—caught her colt, which was already losing weight and wasn't doing her any good either, and locked him in the barn, where in a couple of days he'd forget mama's teats and start gorging himself on barley. The mare we thought would do better unconstrained, so we turned her back in the field to see if she might recover.

This vet, old Doc McPherson, drank. When he was drunk—which was nearly all the time—he was pretty miraculous; his hand shook like a vibrator, but when he let the needle fly it went where he proposed—even into that shifty vein that hides in the neck—whether by aim or magic.

When he was sober his hand shook neither more—it hardly could—nor less, but he looked like a ghost, then, and had the astuteness to be terrified of everything. One Sunday morning when he was sober I saw him clap a handkerchief soaked in chloroform over a colt's nose—what he did wrong I couldn't say, but the colt stopped breathing and never started again. A woman sitting on the fence was the first to notice. "I don't think he's breathing," she said, a little breathless herself. Doc, who was already sitting on the colt's leg, from which he was going to carve away a blemish, looked around and said, "We've got a dead colt, boys. I had a pre-intuition!" That was the word he used, "pre-intuition"—I'm not even sure how it should be spelled. Then he hopped in his car and drove away. How many bars he drove by before he stopped, I don't know. I changed vets after that, but even so we always visited in a friendly enough way when we saw each other, as people do.

But that was later on, and perhaps it's unnecessary to even bring Doc up, since the old roan mare was perfectly capable of dying without him or anyone, and wasn't far from it when I put a bullet in her brain. A trigger, incidentally, if you only arrange everything properly and then concentrate, all but pulls itself—simply a random observation of mine. Even in my salad days, when I used to murder my own beef, I only pulled the trigger. Can you imagine, for example, swinging an ax or a sledge at your fellow creature?

The vet looked at the mare another time or two during the next couple of weeks, though he didn't make a special trip out for it or charge me; he'd shake his head and say, "But you never know," seeming to say at once both that she might live and that she was sure to die. So we let her go as long as seemed reasonable.

5

It was the end of August, and they were still farming away. If I cared to look out the living room window before I went to bed, I could see on the other side of the dark and invisible road dim head-lamps moving over the field: this would be Glenn's tractor. And the next morning at five, although he wouldn't be *out* yet, he'd be up; once in a while I'd catch a glimpse of him emerging from his house in an undershirt to get something or other out of his pickup and carry it back into the kitchen—tobacco possibly, or some bit of equipment he could fool with over his coffee.

At such a busy time you'd have to be a pretty depressed soul not to be thinking eagerly of or daydreaming about fall. Glenn put up hay half the night and went at it again in the early morning. Then, about ten o'clock, when the dew was off, he'd take a break of an hour or even two and drink coffee again—really a lot this time—swizzle it down by the potful. He must have had a bladder like a cow.

This idling time of day was a great pleasure for him, and it was by far the best time to talk to him or ask him a favor. During one of these breaks, not many days after I'd trimmed his jenny, was when I—surely out of some finely calculated swinish cunning—did ask him a favor. But the brute turned me down.

Now I had at the time a high school boy, Dan Eastland, working for me. I used to have a lot of trouble finding a halfway reliable person to do irrigating, barn-sweeping and -cleaning, fence-building, etc. There are good reasons for this: the wages are the lowest of the low; the work is hard, boring, and seasonal to boot; and there's no insurance, no nothing. No one but a fool or a pariah will do such work, usually the latter since, as almost everyone knows, simple foolishness is no obstacle to getting a good job.

But Dan was neither. Being a high school student wanting summer work, he was stuck with me, and he worked for me four summers in a row, saving up his money to go to college so he'd never again have to spend his time so stupidly.

After the first few weeks, I never told him how to do anything—a situation which he rather resented, though he also was amused by what he considered to be my eccentricity.

If I wanted a corral built, for example, I'd tell him to build a corral in a certain place for a certain purpose, of more or less such-and-such a size. From then on he'd do it all—hunting down bargains, everything—in spite of the fact that he thought this way of proceeding peculiar and didn't like it.

He was tall and lean, or, to put it differently, by this time I'd watched him grow from a gangly, slow, shy boy into a somewhat less gangly boy, no less slow and no longer at all shy but mulishly independent. He wore glasses and had a rectangular head. His father was a Swede and spoke English only as a second language. Dan himself spoke slowly and pronounced some words as if he were trying to get a hair out of his mouth. Whether he thought that in doing this he was speaking like his father would be hard to say.

He condescended to me—the way one might to a perfectly harmless dog who has some amusing but incomprehensible habits. There were many instances of this, but only one is important: he thought I was a crazy fool to do the kind of work I did, and more so yet, to like it. In this, sweet reasonableness was all on his side, as I knew even at the time. But because of his own affectation of stupidity, Dan expressed this admirable judgment upon my work in a curious way. He refused to have anything at all to do with the animals. I didn't care about this, since I—in my way—liked to fool with them and didn't like to do much of anything else. But he carried this tendency, or policy, to suspicious extremes. No one could have noticed as little as he seemed to, and being as superstitious as the next fellow, I suspected him of supernatural intelligence—or at least of secretly knowing every horse and cow and all their habits.

He really pretended that these monstrous consumers of grass didn't exist, at least not in the way the rest of us thought they did. True, he couldn't avoid observing that people bought the creatures, sold them, called them by name, doted on them—and this was galling. At best, he would allow that they were tools, part of some elaborate hoax perpetrated by God knows who and fallen for by romantic simpletons. You may think such a conviction would be easy enough to hold to, but after all he was just one insignificant sullen adolescent, and the whole little world of my place was against him. I and my customers and confederates distinguished these beasts one from the other, talked about them, stared endlessly at them, and when one was sick made a great fuss about whether it was going to live or die. Dan was the only one to say us nay in this, and at first it had taken all the independence of mind he could muster to maintain himself. But by now, when he'd been working for me three years, Dan had definitely conquered (himself if no one else), and that's why the following otherwise trivial incident was the more surprising.

One morning—the fatal one—Dan came walking in from the field. I was leading some nag to water, saw him coming, and was mildly curious. He hadn't been out there long enough to move his irrigation settings, which had been running in one place all night and had to be changed (and he wasn't carrying a shovel, as he would have been if he'd been done). I figured he might have had a ditch break and was after a board or some other piece of equipment. But no, he made a swinging motion with his head (like a pair of thieves we'd developed a language); he was looking for me.

"There's a horse out there that looks pretty sick," he said.

This took me aback (though as a matter of pride I didn't show it). Either he'd been watching her like a hawk for weeks and finally divined that her time had come—a frightening notion—or he'd managed to walk by her thirty times during the last two weeks without noticing her at all, and she standing right on the canal bank most of the time, looking like the skeleton of a goat. Both possibilities were unbelievable enough, but the oddest thing was that he'd volunteered to speak about a horse at all. I'd always thought that—as a matter of pride—he'd have walked right over a carcass with no comment but an uncontrollable crinkling of the nose.

I thought to myself, So he's breaking down! "Is there?" I said, with wonderful composure. "Where is she? I'll take a look."

"Right out there by the canal."

"It's a mare, isn't it, Dan? Roan?"

"Could be," he said, and shrugged. He's probably teaching philosophy somewhere right now.

I walked out and looked at her. She didn't and in fact couldn't look much worse than she had the night before. Well, it was time to put an end to it. To the extent that I could be amused, it amused me that Dan had called the shot. On my way back to the barn I met him walking out with a canvas dam rolled up on his shoulder—whether he really was going to use the dam or just didn't want me to think he'd come in merely to tell me about the horse, I've never decided. We met in a little fenced-off lane where the barnyard and two fields came together. I said, "Yeah, she's in a bad way all right, Dan. Help me drive her down here, will you? All you've got to do is walk behind her."

We trailed her down the canal bank into the lane and closed the gate. "She's one old mare no one would've corralled afoot a month ago," I said.

He didn't answer or even look at her that I could tell. "She's the one that's had sleeping sickness," I said, still trying.

"Oh yeah?" he said, as if sleepily.

"Uh-huh—I want to put her in here so the tallow man can get close to her with his truck."

"Tallow man," he said stupidly. But God knows if it was a question or what.

"I'm going to go across the road and borrow a gun."

"Are you going to shoot her?" he said—naively, almost like a child; it surprised me, but I didn't weaken.

"Can't put her in the deadwagon alive," I said, "so I guess I'm elected, unless you'd like to do it for me?"

"No thanks," he said—laconic. Damn these wretches who won't hold to their convictions! He pretended they were posts, but if I'd asked him to shoot a bullet into a post for me, he'd have done it soon enough. Well, at least he was found out. But I was irritated. I'd hoped he might make up for his apparent sentimental lapse by pulling off a bit of bravado and saying something like "I don't care" or "Doesn't make any difference to me who shoots her," a mistake I'd

have been quick to take advantage of. "No thanks," he says, just as
if I'd offered him a second helping of spinach! For a dollar-fifty an
hour you can't even get a horse shot! Well, to hell with him and
worse luck for me, I thought. It crossed my mind that I could pay
old Doc to do it—but no, I still had some pride. . . . If I could get
him to drive out ostensibly for something else and then . . . but no.
I fussed around with some job or other and managed to pass about
an hour. (Dan, incidentally, disappeared to the far end of the place
and didn't reappear until later in the day.) I sneaked a look: she was
still there. I'd had some crazy hope that she might have lain down
and died, of her own free will, so to speak.

6

Glenn was drinking coffee. He gave me some, and I said I had a
mare I had to kill and wondered if I could borrow a gun.

"Sure you can," he said, and immediately got up and took one out
of the cabinet and got some shells out of a drawer and laid both gun
and shells on the sideboard—we were in the kitchen—and sat back
down. "That's a shame," he said. "What's wrong with the mare?"
He said this in a gentle, deferential way, the tone—carefully more
sympathetic than curious—in which you ask about someone's personal troubles.

I told him that she had sleeping sickness and how it was that I
hadn't happened to vaccinate her. Then it occurred to me, as I
heard myself speak, that he had three or four horses and that he almost certainly hadn't vaccinated them. There'd been no cases in this
part of the valley for twenty years. Now mine. Sleeping sickness is
carried by mosquitoes, and obviously one infecting mosquito in the
neighborhood indicated more. I knew he must be ruminating about
this himself, though as a matter of politeness he could hardly say so.

So I offered to vaccinate his horses for him. And out of either
kindness or diabolical cunning I managed to put it in a way that
made refusal difficult. I told him I had a few doses of vaccine left,
and that it would spoil before next mosquito season anyway and
might as well be used up. I said that if he could get them in the cor-

ral I'd do it that very afternoon, wouldn't take ten minutes.

This tempted him, by its very reasonableness, though he hated to be beholden to anyone for anything. "Be a lot of bother," he said.

"Not for me," I said. "Nothing to it."

"Well, better to shoot them for it than because of it," he said, giving in.

"I've got one that'll vouch for that," I said.

We finally agreed that he'd have his kids run the horses into the corral that afternoon, and I'd come over in the evening and we'd vaccinate them. Then I got up to go. He tried to delay me, and actually offered to show me a few new coins. He collected them, and one evening when he'd had several people over, we'd gathered around the table and looked at them—after supper when he was naturally in an expansive mood. Now I found it somehow fetching that he wanted to show them to me again, and in the middle of a workday morning at that. I looked, and in my mood hardly saw what I was shown.

That evening the collection itself had meant nothing to me, and I'd simply made polite remarks; but now I was affected in spite of myself by the way he moved the coins around gently and delicately with his fat, well-nicked fingers, his head bent over as far as his big bull neck would allow, and his face shining. (Farmers—even those who aren't fat—tend to shine regularly, I've noticed, when they're indoors drinking coffee, no matter what the time of day or year.)

He put back the beloved coins and showed me how to work the gun, loading it for me and putting it on safety. I watched. He handled the gun affectionately. I looked at it, and I looked at his stolid face: fondness expressed there unmistakably. Well, even brutes are fond, but what are they fond of? And after all, how they loved to hunt! I began calculating to myself rapidly: *he must feel in my debt.* I'd sweated over his jenny, and now I'd as good as vaccinated his horses (the vaccine alone would have cost him twenty dollars, and I was pretty sure he knew it).

All this was running through my mind in no very clear way. He held out the gun, offering it to me and expecting me to reach out and take it from him; I expected the same myself, but I drew back instead, though only slightly. He put it down on the table between us and we both acted as if nothing had happened. But his face had already begun to change: to close and to grow longer. From sheer nervousness I clenched my hands, put my fists on the table, and leaned forward on my knuckles, looking at him and yet never able to get the gun out of my vision; and I said—again without knowing what I was going to do while at the same time knowing I was going to do something wrong: "You wouldn't want to kill her for me, would you?"

His face shut like a door. Before, when he'd held out the gun and I'd drawn back, he'd been puzzled and hurt, but now he was furious.

Even before he spoke, I blushed.

"I have to shoot my own," he said.

You can't just vanish. I picked up the gun. "I'll bring it right back, Glenn," I said.

"All right. Just take the shells out of it and lay it on the table if no one's here."

That there would be no one there I had no doubt. And I was glad of it.

But how could we avoid each other? So it was a very good thing that he was a sensible man. Though he never warmed up to me again, he always managed to be civil.

Sterling's Calf

It was early and still dark; Sterling was getting up. He sneaked out from under the covers. He didn't want his wife to wake. While he was just pulling up his pants, he saw the set of car lights coming down the road. It was a public road, but he was curious who it was.

The lights weren't tracking quite straight. Was this a fact or produced by his sleepy early-morning eyes? He kept watching. He began to watch so hard that he had to stop trying to button his pants. He never took his eyes off the car, which was certainly wandering.

The car veered so that it looked as if it was coming in the bedroom. The sound of wire ripping, a thud or two, and it still wasn't in the bedroom, so he knew it had come to rest in the pasture, just under the window. There had been another flutter of activity out there too, so faintly perceived that he didn't know whether he'd seen movement in the dark or heard it.

A little later he guessed at what it was. Five or six calves often bedded down at night right there by the fence. He guessed they had probably been there asleep and must have scattered like a nest of struck billiard balls.

That was what he guessed. And later on, when he found a calf (the blind one) hiding in a ditch with a broken hind leg, then he saw how good his guess was. But that was later on, when it was light and he was out and around.

Now his wife was awake for sure. Well, it would give her something to thank God for, Sterling thought, that the car hadn't driven right on into the bedroom, that the boy wasn't hurt, etc. There was no end to the things you could thank God for, if you ever once got started.

By the time Sterling got out there, the boy was out of his car, standing and looking the side of it that was bashed in. It turned out it wasn't his car but his father's, and this was his first day on a job at a dairy down the road, and he hadn't even kept awake long enough to get there.

Sterling led him into the kitchen and they mopped the blood off his face and put a band-aid on him. He looked dazed but from the looks of him that was probably the way he always looked, more or less. Sterling called the father, who sounded as if this was exactly what he had expected: as if he had known all the time that this was what would happen to his car and had just been lying there waiting for the phone to ring. Sterling told him that if he would just go down to the farm supply first thing this morning and pay for a roll of page-wire and two packages of steel posts, then Sterling would forget the whole thing. Get the heavy-duty stuff, Sterling told him.

When he built it the first time he'd been thinking of calves, but now he wanted to deflect cars.

That fence had been as rotten and rusty as you could imagine, so this was a break: he was going to gain fifty dollars or so.

Sterling got the boy back in his car and out on the road. He tried to remind himself that he was a boy once, too. He'd heard people say that: "I was a boy once myself!" and he had great faith in sayings, or maybe no faith at all but anyway he liked them. He looked hard at the boy's face and decided that he, Sterling, had never looked or been quite so stupid as that; but he had been a boy, hadn't he? Must have been. Actually he couldn't remember having ever been much different than he was.

He tried to remember doing something boyish. How about when he used to leave his horse saddled overnight so that he wouldn't have to waste time saddling him in the morning? Well, it still seemed worth trying, if he hadn't already. Either I never was a boy or I still am one, he thought.

Then it occurred to him that what he always told people—I'm just a boy come over from the old country (even if I do own four thousand mother cows and the land and leases to carry them)—was really so.

He watched the car receding back the way it had come. It was still dark enough that you could see the lights on in the neighbor's house and light enough now that you could see smoke coming out the chimney. Suddenly several thoughts seemed to meet, like colliding shadows. It was Wednesday. For him it was sale day: they started selling cattle at one o'clock. He never missed it. He'd build the fence tomorrow. But he'd better saddle a horse and move the calves to another field, or they'd be straying through the gap and out onto the road.

He used to tromp his own fences down, so that the cattle would get out and eat the tall grass along the sides of the public road—the long pasture, he called it. But that was before they had a phone. Now you couldn't keep the neighbors from calling every fifteen minutes to tell you your cattle were out—and if your wife was in the house, that was the end of it. God only knew the trouble they caused—neighbors, phones, and wives.

It was a long-haired, potbellied little orphan calf, the sorriest animal that Sterling owned, and blind as a mole. That's why it had been the last to try and get out of the way; the others had seen the car lights coming at them.

Last spring he'd given a dollar for the calf. No one had even wanted to bid, because it didn't look as if it would even survive the auction and get home. But it turned out to be a trying little thing and had managed to steal milk and keep alive. Lived, but hardly grew. So that Sterling often wished he'd never bought it, even for a dollar, because after all it probably ate as much grass as a good one. Now the calf was standing in the ditch and quivering, packing one leg. Well, if he had to lose one he'd as soon it was this one.

Then he remembered the insurance: of course the cattle were not insured, but animals struck by cars—that was different. After he got the calf up to the barn, he called the agent.

The agent said they needed a certificate from the slaughterhouse saying that the calf was dead and wouldn't make meat, and an estimate of value.

"There's not much to him," Sterling said. "Any more. There's not much to him any more. I don't believe they could make much of an estimate. Do you see what I mean? Could you tell me how big a rain cloud was, if you only saw the puddles it left?"

"I see," said the agent. "They'll just have to do what they can."

"Tell me what you think of this," Sterling said. "What if I just average my other calves of the same age and come up with a figure? He came right out of the same field."

"I don't know. That sounds possible, I suppose, though it's not regular. Mail us the death certificate and the estimates and we'll try to get a check out to you as soon as we can, Mr. Green."

"I'll bring the certificate by myself this morning and wait for the check," Sterling said.

"I'm not sure—"

"Why's that? Are you overdrawn? I'll give you the name of a banker too, if the company's up against it. I'll bring the calf too, if you like. I'll put the pieces in a bag and bring him in so that you can run an estimate on him yourself. I don't want to put anything over on you."

The man laughed nervously, for a long time.

"What kind of meat do you think he'll make?" Sterling said to the man at the packinghouse.

"He wouldn't make any for me, would he for you, Sterling?"

"Make me out a death cetificate on him, could you? I've got some insurance to collect."

The man said there was a five-dollar charge for the certificate and it included the favor of killing him and getting him out of the way.

"All right," Sterling said, and he was about to unload him when he looked through the slats and it dawned on him that if being orphaned and blinded and run over hadn't killed him yet, this broken leg might not either. Especially since his legs hadn't much but hide to carry anyway. Three ought to be good enough for that. "I believe I'll take him home and feed him to my dogs," Sterling said, "but I suppose I'll have to pay you for the certificate regardless."

The man blinked once and said he guessed that was fair enough. "You people make it hard for a poor boy to get by," Sterling said, laughing and paying for his piece of paper.

He stopped at the drugstore and bought some plaster of paris and a lot of gauze. When he got home he gathered up a bucket of water and some sticks and set the leg and casted it and closed the calf up in the barn. After that he went back downtown and spent an hour sitting in the insurance office. He didn't care much for that, and it was true they might have mailed it. But he didn't like to give them time to think. If they believed he wouldn't leave, they'd pay him off to get rid of him. Besides, he was a big customer. On the way out of town he picked up his wire and posts. By the time he got to the auction yard, the sale was just getting started.

Sterling sat down in one of the padded chairs in the front row—the one they kept reserved for him—and stared between the cables at an old cow. He heard the bidding and read most of her life story on her hide, but his head was full of figures. It was too bad he hadn't milked the boy's father for the calf. He should have made him pay for it. Of course he could have called him back and made him, but Sterling had feelings against that: he wasn't one to try to rearrange fate. He'd got fifty dollars worth of new fencing material and the price of an average fall calf—one hundred and seventy-five dollars altogether—and he'd lost a couple of rotten posts, spent five dollars for the death certificate and four for the plaster of paris and gauze, and he'd killed half a day. These figures penetrated his brain with such intensity that he almost forgot to notice who bought the first cow and for how much.

Early Winter

The meadow or, as they called it, the swamp was a ranch in itself, some sixty miles off the pavement and a long hundred from town. And the swamp or meadow, big as it was (it would summer a thousand cows and grow the hay to winter them too), was just a pock on the desert, the junipered high desert with its big river cuts and occasional badlands of broken black rock that you could hardly lead a horse through and which they called devils' gardens; the meadow was nothing but a pock in the desert that ran changingly on and filled the big meeting corners of three states.

On the steep at the edge of the meadow was a set of corrals and a barn, a gas-motored power plant, and a good house. For more or less than six months of the year the road was passable, though it would go any time it rained, even in the summer. And there was a telephone that worked a surprising amount of the time as long as it wasn't storming. If you were riding the desert you'd run into that thin bare wire that staggered from tree to tree to pole as randomly as if it belonged there, and I mean really run into it if you weren't watching, because often it was low enough to unhorse you.

Fall was more than with them. Spring calves, big now, had sucked the fat off their mothers with the milk. The good was gone out of the feed. It was come-home time. Little groups of range cattle were finding their ways into the come-home lanes or just wandering down the fence lines, walking along with their heads down, spoiled to preferring a winter of hay, captivity, mud, and tractor-broke snow to the risky pickings of wintering out. Coming down randomly, just the way the Indians in that part of the country used to, where they would bunch up in the lowlands, fifty together in those close and stinking communal houses with the chiefs sitting closest to the air holes, and argue over how many months of winter were left. Ben watched the cattle as he drove along, he couldn't help it.

Behind him swayed his potbellied mare; his saddle was cinched to the racks. Beside him on the seat and floor of the truck cab was a whole pile of stuff: bridles, brushes, halters and lass-ropes, medicines for doctoring cattle, a raincoat, chaps, rubber boots made to fit a stirrup, matches, a furred cap, and so on.

At home he had dried up the one cow and turned the nurse calves on the other, and he had fixed a place where the two skim-milk pigs—one he was fattening for his brother and the other for himself—could get in out of the weather. The irrigation water was shut out of the ditches clear back at the county locks. His fields were frozen. There was enough old growth standing to hold his cattle for a month (after that he'd have to pitch hay). In other words, there wasn't much to do outdoors but keep an eye out. His wife had no hard outdoor chores to do, and they wouldn't be owing to his brother for anything except to keep a watch after Ben's cattle, to look in on Marian and drink her coffee.

At home: that farmland, fenced and cross-fenced, square as a house—as the house it owned—and flat as a table, with its touchy domestic grasses and shedding poplars. Bare branches, shed out now; a wintry place it was, home, already it was looking wintry, and when it was wintry it was dead and sad. The desert though was various, rolling and live. It escaped the seasons and penetrated the horizons, jumped its own gorges and flew on. He supposed that's why even those sudden gorges and sheer cliffs were only called cuts and breaks. Because the desert belittled its own monuments. No landmark really broke or season really killed it. Juniper, wild plum, and sage—they shed no leaves; paw a foot of snow off a clump of bunchgrass and you'll find it just as green as summer would have.

Ten miles in he passed a big weathered house together with a big roughly leveled field. Twenty years ago a dry-farmer had failed there. Now it was Sterling's, who'd bought up so much of this country, and the house was fenced off with a good, bright, four-wire fence, to keep Sterling's cattle from worrying the place down, as a cow is likely to run a nail in her foot, or even to wander inside and get in a tight spot she can't get out of. It's odd though, Ben thought, to see a house fenced like that, four bright wires all around, with no break, no gate.

He passed Goose Lake, round as a dollar, seeming not to reflect the clear blue sky but to glitter opaquely with a kind of tinfoil energy of its own. In its center a wooden float, broken, which the P-38s used to practice diving down on fifteen years before. That was how the float got lopped off, too, he'd heard. There was one that, as if to prove its excellent aim, never pulled up. Imagine that, Goose Lake's only wave. But looking at the lake he couldn't imagine it. It could only have entered splashless, as in a dream.

Beyond it, a real landmark: the cylindrical mountain, Horse Cock, the same from every side, with its peculiarly convex mesa and swollen underlip, like a flashlight on end or a cake that swelled over and out of the pan it was baked in, a muffin—but more like its namesake, the tumescent penis of a stallion, than any of those. And some in-between in the Forest Service had changed the name to Horse Mountain when it came time to make a map.

He widened the road a little on the curves, as if he was trying to outrun his own dust, but there wasn't any. The old mare stood behind his shoulder, spraddle-legged, tilting wide outside with the brown eye of experience, a little frightened, gauging through the slats. She stumbled and he saw her eye. Well, he slowed himself down. If he could just get it through his head that he was being paid by the day now rather than the mile, and that there was no reason to hurry. So used had he become to hauling cattle for so much a mile. Certainly he didn't mean to overwork himself or his truck or his mare for Sterling. Sterling, who always set before a man more than he could possibly get done, hoping that way to surprise him into turning an extra lick or two over his hours and wages.

Forty miles in he crossed water, a young creek in the center of a broad and shallow wash; a slab had been laid over the crossing, so the only part of this desert that was paved was the thirty feet under water. Above that on the far side was a herder's camp, a box of a trailer with a pin hitch that would push a car more directions than the car would ever pull it, if you dared it on the highway. Parked now under a tree, and in front of it a big dust-encrusted woman. Well, any woman was a rarity in a sheep camp. Still, she could have bathed. Probably she was so used to dry camps that she didn't know what to make of a watered one.

Near her, a hobbled and saddled horse. It was not long after noon. He figured that a band of sheep was probably over some rise with a dog or two and that the sheepherder would be asleep in the trailer or under a tree behind it. He thought these things idly, for no reason. No, the herder would be inside this day, which had too much sting to it even at noon to let a man sleep away from a blanket or fire, though you couldn't really call it cold.

The woman looked at him with no show of interest, sitting dumb and expressionless, though he could tell by the deadness of the tire tracks in the road that he was the first to pass here in at least a day or two and more likely a week.

He thought, Well, you might have to be out here quite a while before you'd want her, but when you did she'd be there. No matter who was chasing who she'd never outrun you, or even wander very far from camp, let alone leave on you. . . .

The road fell down over a steep, as off a ridge, but he'd been traveling flat for a hundred miles; the road fell down the bank, dropping some hundred feet in a quarter of a mile, and the meadow was there, as round as anything five miles across that isn't pure water can be. The house was flung out in a pocket at the foot of the hill and below it a maze of privy and pumphouse and calf sheds and the housing of the generator and a sorry tangle of little fences that kept in and separated a milk cow or two and the house calves—or had: it was all empty now, and below that a good barn and some pole corrals big and solid enough that you could work a thousand cattle at a time through them, or a few hundred horses, but it was all empty now, not even a saddle horse around, though farther out the meadow was dotted, and anywhere you looked on the desert you could see a cow or two among the junipers.

The place was empty now because Sterling's man had died and it was hard to get another one. They'd stay a few days or a week and leave. Rare the single man who would stay long way out here, but Sterling had come up with one who had stayed a long time, even if he was having trouble coming up with another.

Ben had ridden out mornings after cattle with Sterling's man, a half-deaf old fellow not much more than five feet tall. All alone he'd stayed out here for years, apparently having nothing better to do until he died, which he'd finally gone ahead and done last winter, though he'd gone to town to do that. Shorty was his name and Ben had ridden with him, the one as unused to speaking as the other was to shouting, so that little was said. Except once when he told Ben to go down in the mosquitoes and move a sixteen-foot canvas dam, Ben had managed to yell, "If you want it done, do it yourself. I take all my orders from the man who makes out the checks."

The one person who would talk to Shorty, and had talked to him, was Sterling. They'd stand shouting at each other, Shorty telling Sterling where there was a sick cow, which waters were wet and which dry and where there were too many cattle and not enough feed, or the other way around, or where a man might borrow a chain harrow, and then Sterling would tell Shorty what to do about it. On and on they'd go, standing eyeball to bellybutton and shouting, the two giants Ben called them, the big giant and the little giant.

In the house, on a yellow wall above a narrow iron bedstead, a list had been nailed. Ben looked at it. Imagine Shorty going to sleep every night under—living under—a list of chores. He wouldn't have forgotten what he was there for, that was sure. To ride with Shorty had been the next thing to being alone, and in fact at those times Ben, if he'd had his rathers, would rather have been alone, had wished he was alone. Now he wished him life, just for the company.

Ben rattled around the old place. What was he doing here, anyway? A question not of sense—he knew what he was doing here.

Part of the trouble was that the place was too big, he thought. House, outbuildings, barn, the roar of the big gas-engined generator that he'd just fired up, roaring now like a tremendous dose of silence, like all the silence of the empty corners of three states buzzing, like a fly in your ear. Even Shorty had no more than camped here all those years. It was a place for a family, hired man, hay crew, a few teams of horses. Yet you couldn't get a family to stay here either. The kids couldn't get to school, for one thing. And what woman nowadays would stand being snowed, frozen, and mudded in from more or less Thanksgiving until more or less the first of May?

Ben went back out of the house and hayed the mare and wired the gate shut so she'd be there in the morning. It was colder here than at home, and the long ride hadn't done her any good, so that her long hair which had already "come in winter" was standing on end like the fur of a dead rabbit. He looked at the clouds blowing up over Oregon and opened the barn door for the mare so that she could get in out of the weather if she liked.

There had been a family here, before Shorty, which was why the place was what it was, the house and all: two brothers, one with a wife. And they were the kind to tough it out and like it, thrive on it, though they never owned it.

Well they were long gone now, he thought, the only sign of them being an extravagant wood-stove, the kind with a confusing lot of vents and dampers and heat-shifting levers and two warming ovens above the firebox and two regular ovens below it and a trash burner, and weighing so much that it had sunk on one side through the kitchen floor. Now mice and even chipmunks went back and forth through the hole.

Ben shook a spider out of the coffeepot, banged a few sticks of wood together and built a fire in a corner of the stove, knocked the cobwebs off the broom and swept the kitchen, ran some of the rust out of the water pipes and filled the coffeepot and sat down and stared at the wall, putting him in mind of other walls he'd stared at. Outside it got dark. What was he doing here?

Money, yes, and that was reason enough to come. But the answer really had nothing to do with the question. What in the world was he doing here? He'd spent enough nights alone in his life and even one more was too many. Besides that, it was somehow silly, with her sitting there alone and lonely and he here. And her worse off, when he thought of it, because she would be the victim of Sterling's wife or

Clyde's wife or someone's, who would insist on sitting with her, which she wouldn't want but would accept.

All the walls he had stared at: walls of line camps and construction camps and road-building camps and trail-cutting camps and logging and mining camps, not to mention the shacks and cabins and hotels and rooms in people's houses and yards. Brick, stone, tin, canvas, cardboard even. Worst the thin walls of hotels, stained at the level of the bed from the spittle and semen of men more single than he had ever been, penetrated by the coughing and pure terrors of men out of wine and coming down, men more married—at least more hopelessly married—to the bottle than he ever was. And when he sat straight up in bed out of sleep in the middle of the night to the tune of that! Yes, and at that time of night in those places alone your skin gets pretty thin and your self-respect along with it.

He hardly marked when it started to snow.

He remembered one Labor Day's drunk, the end of a great drunk, of almost a whole summer's drunk really. Because hadn't he been either drunk or on his way to getting sober (he never made it), from June to September? That was the summer when his ranch, the ranch he'd saved up six thousand dollars to lease and stock, was going belly up. But that isn't quite the way he was thinking of it now. He was simply picturing the end of a great drunk, himself up on a great black rock at a Labor Day celebration, driving steel with a ten-pound hammer, and he smiled a little as he thought of it. He stared at one spot on the wall and he saw that one picture. It remained at the center, but other incidents circled and fed it.

Himself on the rock wearing a plaster cast, and he thought for an instant of the day in the spring of the year when he took a flyer off a spilling wagonload of meadow hay. Flung he was, and crushed his ankle when he lit. He remembered making the doctor set it with him awake. "How much pain can you stand?" the man asked. "What I have to." Because he didn't want to be unconscious and them messing with him. Especially strangers, especially doctors. He would no more have let them put him to sleep than he would have fallen asleep in a barber chair with a razor on his neck. Of course he knew there was no rhyme or reason to it, that they would go on and do what they would do anyway, and that finally, awake or asleep, he would have to just go on and let them.

He remembered raking a lot of hay with a one-horse buckrake, his plaster leg propped straight out in front of him on a forked stick. The hay, he even remembered, had gone shelly from lying around too long in the sun while he tried to borrow a baler, so that most of the grain spilled back onto the ground, and the next tenant would have a good crop of volunteer oats at the expense of Ben's hay. And he remembered playing housewife to the hay crew, so that when they were getting up at four he was getting up at two-thirty to build them breakfast. Right down to the butane stove and the kerosene lantern and the radio turned to KXLA, which would bring in western music all the way from Los Angeles until about daylight, when it began to fade. . . . And in the evenings he would imagine them, the others, down at the river, their bodies drawn along by the current, the water pulling at the fine, burning chaff, while he chafed under his plaster and tossed grapes to the dog from the back steps.

When all the hay was in he'd begun to drink. There was nothing else to do. Every Sunday they'd catch another laying hen and eat her. Sometimes he could dance like a sound-legged man. One day the barn burned; the shingles glided flaming all over the hillside like runaway kites and they went chasing them and he prayed for it all to burn, every tree of it.

Then one night he woke to the insistent yapping of the dog and when he got to the barnyard heard the frantic squawking of a hen and finally found her with a cow standing on her leg, the cow too placid or uncaring or dumb to move, and he thought that was how it should be, not a weasel in the henhouse but a cow standing on a chicken, on his ranch.

The black rock on an iron-ribbed wagon. On Labor Day the whiskey had flowed. Someone had managed to have the rock loaded onto the wagon and towed it downtown with a tractor. Jamestown—that had been a town to fit him then; the man he was then it fit wonderfully well, the Mother Lode dead a hundred years almost but the town still a good Saturday-night town. Fourteen bars and a grocery store and a hotel, and the people loose and at loose ends, tied and not very tightly to those old slow-diers, the mills and the dwindling woods and mined-out mines and sheeped-out hills. . . . Someone— a one-eyed trader drunker than he was—had been fool enough to hold the drill for him while he swung at it with the hammer (hit it, too), his plaster cast propped some way he couldn't remember. Drunken fools. And right now sitting in this kitchen with his coffee boiling over, probably the first time he'd ever thought of it since and not been ashamed of the spectacle.

He got ready to go to bed. You had to go out to the generator to turn it on, but to cut the power you had only to flick a switch in the kitchen: just like uptown, except that the light and sound going at once was a shock. So that then, for a time all he could hear standing in the dark was the roar backward in time.

He turned to the window and watched it snow, and then the roar went away and he began to hear—sounding the way sleep might sound—the soft loud hush of snowing.

II

The next morning when he went out Ben couldn't say he was surprised: he'd had a good notion through the night of how heavily it was snowing. Yet as he stood on the porch pulling on his gloves he couldn't help being astonished by the landscape. The meadow and the desert—all snow.

On the top edge of the open barn door, on every top fence rail and balanced on the top of each post were the most symmetrical, delicate peaks of unbroken snow. Even the four-pronged barbs on the wire were fluffy, or looked like big crystals.

The cows and calves were already trompling and making the trackless meadow imperfect. Irregular patches of snow, melting and steaming, rode on their backs. Ben buckled up his rubber boots and stepped off into it.

When he went to hay his mare he stopped and leaned on the fork and hooked an elbow over her warm hip and said a few admiring words about her not being about to get her old back wet—which he might never have done if they hadn't been stuck out here all alone together. A magpie walked out of the barn before him and fluttered onto a rail.

Ben went out too. The magpie walked the fence, kicking off snow, too close to him, walking and cawing and kicking off snow. Cawing, two-toned, puffed-up and gaudy. They were vile enough any time, but every winter especially they grew impertinent. This one was rushing the season to boot. So that he went to the trouble to work a rock out from under the snow and flung it.

It missed the bird and hit the fence, scattering snow, and made a thwack that gave a start to every cow for a hundred yards. Even the mare jumped and snorted. All sorts of exaggerated spookiness spread on across the white meadow: tails and hackles stood straight up on end as if the dry air was really electric. But the bird only hopped a little farther from him and kept on with its nasty cawing.

His job of work had changed. He could see that the weather was now going to do the most part of his cow-gathering for him. Twos and threes of them with their big calves trailing along behind were winding down off the slopes, dark among the whitened junipers everywhere. The weather had given him a new job too, and one he cared for less. The feed on the meadow—feed that usually would have carried the cattle another month, until it had a good ordinary right to snow—all that was inundated now. So he had to feed hay. He could see the stacks, the big stacks of loose summer-cut hay dotting the big meadow, each with a fence around it to keep the cattle off. And he'd seen a sled, parked dry and cobwebby in the shed. And he knew where the harness hung. So now what he had to do was to wrangle a team and go to pitching hay. A job he cared a lot less for than riding after cattle, though he didn't care so much for that any more either. Well, it didn't pay to give it much thought. Besides, he did like having to give himself up to the weather. He began wondering where he might find a team.

He knew that Sterling had a few workhorses turned loose down here somewhere, or did have, and Ben tried to estimate which way across the unfenced desert they might have wandered.

While the mare ate, he went back to the house and softened some coffee with canned milk and poured some water into the top of a flour sack and squeezed together some dough and rolled it out and cut off some biscuits with a water glass and baked them. The kitchen was warmed to the corners with the fire he'd built when he got up and his coffee'd done a good deal of boiling while he was out, even though he'd left it on the corner of the stove.

When he was done he threw a saddle on her and rode out, a few strips of jerky in his pocket, remembering that when he was a young man he'd always packed himself a good lunch and was wanting at it by ten o'clock, while now he would ride out with an ounce or two of jerky and as often as not would find it still in his pocket when he rode in at night.

He had no real notion of where the horses were, and all sign was covered. Idly he began looking for them in his mind's eye, picturing them in this place and that, some of the places being so far away that he hated to think of them really being there. Until, giving in to some chance mixture of indecision and intuition, he took off northeast and came on them three hours' straight ride later—noon it was. "I must be living right," he said when he saw them, half a dozen big-footed workhorses, who threw up their big craggy heads at the sight of him and started a trail back toward the ranch, glad enough not to have to paw snow for a meal, he supposed, only needing someone to start them, to jog their memories a little, to remind them there was such a thing as captivity and a haypile. In the spring of the year it would have been another story: they would have been trying to break back over the top of him every chance they saw, trying to stay in the country, out among the wild ones and the new grass. But not now.

He let them go. They broke trail for him, heading straight for the ranch. It was a shining day but a short one, and cold. He pounded his gloved hands on the saddle horn until he knocked a little sting into them. When his feet began to lose feeling he got off the mare and walked. He was afoot, coming along a ridge, when he saw the horses below him trotting right along and then suddenly split from their direction, taking a hard break too, right up a drifted gully, bounding through deep snow. And that surprised him, until he looked down again and saw what they'd seen or got wind of: a big bull, stretched out dead with the turkey vultures on it and around it.

Their hard eyes snapped at him. They already had it half undressed. "Well there's one old baloney bull who'll never make Chicago now," he said. Then he looked around and saw a good windfall and decided to thaw out.

He knocked a little snow off the deadfall: he shook it and peeked in among the branches. It was a regular good nest of twigs and sticks, besides the well-weathered branches of the tree that began it. If he'd had any sense at all he would have pulled out some of the sticks, dug a hole in the snow, and built a small fire. Instead he peeled a handful of tinder, set it inside, and just set the whole thing afire.

It flamed up big, as how could he help but know it would? Too hot to stand near, and his feet were what was cold. He had to squat off at some distance. He watched the vultures. They rated and gauged him too, snatching their heads away from their work, cocking their heads toward him with their black snapping eyes working on him. With strings of flesh in their mouths—they never stopped stringing flesh.

His fire flamed up bigger and hotter; after all, it was a whole tree. His face stung and glowed with fresh heat and embarrassment. He decided he must have been a little out of his mind when he lit it.

Then he became preoccupied with a whole series of trifling occurrences that he felt he was taking notice of for the first time, though they must have actually entered his imagination with great purity and force just minutes before:

the surprised head of the first workhorse tossing up—ears pressed forward, popeyed, nostrils as wide and still as teacups, pure attention against the blank white land;

the reins, wrapped around his glove, tensing and slacking as he leads the mare along the ridge, him trying to stalk, bent-kneed, from one big new hoofprint to the next;

the veined pallor of his hands when he ungloves; the kindness or gentleness visible in the very shape of those worked and weathered hands of his;

the squeak of his boots, his rubber boots, against the fine dry snow, an electric and lonely sound in the dry air until he hears the timbred voice, reminding him of a musical instrument, say "Well there's one old baloney bull who'll never make Chicago now."

While he was recontemplating these things a coyote slipped up to the carcass. She was already working it when Ben finally took notice. Life was doing her no favors, you could just glance at her and see that. Her swaying string of hairy teats were the biggest part of her. He guessed she had a litter of big summer pups hidden somewhere, and probably fat, who kept the meat sucked off her old bones. "You could do with a weaning too, couldn't you sister," he said, thinking of the cows and their big spring calves.

His fire wasn't blossoming the way it had been. He got closer and closer to it, until he was heated up all the way through. For the first time in several hours he could feel his ulcer churn. He imagined it as a coal, a good live coal heating him outward. He imagined himself as a candidate for spontaneous combustion, like a load of green hay, boiling secret and airless at the center until it goes off. That amused him, even the words amused him—spontaneous combustion. He watched the birds and went on hating them with an excellent, hot little hatred, so pure and concentrated that he could have almost located and extracted it too, like an object, like a coal.

When he got on his mare he left his right hand ungloved and took down his summertime lass-rope, which in this weather had gone stiff as a board, and as he rode down off the ridge he built a little creaky loop. He'd have loved nothing so much as to have lucked it on one of those vultures just one time, just to change the look in those eyes one time. But they flapped on out of reach as coolly as they did everything else, not even bothering to fly. The bitch coyote, though, was appparently ravening. By the time she looked up and saw him coming, he was already closer than he should have been. She panicked and leaped out in a squeeze between the mare and the bull, right past him. And the loop that he threw just for the hell of it, to see if he could, because he'd never roped a coyote and because it was ready in his hand—the loop whipped up around her neck and he sucked the slack out of it in one motion and snatched her right around out of the air.

She flung herself back against it, shutting off her own air and striking and snapping mostly at nothing, because the rope was at best a blur and most of the time above her and out of her sight alto-gether.

He had to laugh at himself. He'd only wanted to catch her, not to be tied to her. Now he remembered what he already knew, that some things are easier to get into than out of. He wanted his rope back. Anyway he figured he had more use for it than she did. There was no use in her running herself more ragged than she already was, trying to get away from it, or getting herself tied for all time to a bush.

She was surely gaunt. He'd roped lots of soggy little calves not half as tall as she was, and not many of them could he have held with the rope just in his bare hand the way he easily could her. All long hair. Even throwing the fit that she was, she felt to him like a jackrabbit on the line, which was a sorry way to start a winter, that thin.

She wouldn't hang back and choke herself long, he knew, before she'd be making a desperate run at him and his mare, and maybe really get him in a jackpot. So he tied the rope to the saddle horn and tied the mare's head to the rope so that she, if she lost her nerve, couldn't turn tail and run off. Then he started pretty gingerly down the line, stopping to pull his glove on, cursing himself all the way for his foolishness, and wondering why a man his age would still play pranks.

As he came on she hauled back harder and wilder, her head flap-ping and popping, tongue out, until when he was about six feet from her she jumped toward him as she was bound to, trying to get at him or by him, he couldn't tell. But he had the rope in his hand and stepped aside and snatched the slack from her and popped her side-ways, so that she flew to the end of it again like a cork on a string. And while she still suffered from that he managed to get to her and run the arch of his foot right down the rope and hard onto her throat and head, though not without getting his boot slashed. Then he had her pinned, her head right under his foot, squashed down into the snow, one eye bugging out of its socket not at him or anything. The rest of her flopped two or three times like a beached fish, and that's all. She quit. He saw that her teats had been actually sucked raw, and suddenly he imagined a pup trying to sneak up and suck her in the dark, and in his mind she roars with pain and rage, and her teeth flash.

He wondered if he was giving her too much. He didn't want to kill her, and he didn't want to get his hand bitten, especially when he saw that she'd gone through both of his boots, the rubber and the leather, clear to his sock. When at last he lifted his foot off her, she didn't move. He pulled her toward the mare, stuck his gloved hand between the rope and her furred neck, and pulled off the loop.

Ben thought he should see whose bull it was. He couldn't find a brand showing, so he looped the hind legs and took a turn or two around the saddle horn and rolled him. It was Sterling's all right. And he'd like to be able to tell him what the bull died of, as a good cowboy should. You couldn't tell anything with this new snow. You couldn't tell whether he'd lain here a long time and just wasted away slowly, down sick, or if he'd just lain down here and died, or if he'd suffered and torn up the ground in his pain, or what. So he tried to do some pathology: looked at the tongue, the eyes, the feet, the liver—couldn't tell a thing. It looked like a good active bull. His hooves were slick and hard as a new black ax, as if he'd done a lot of traveling over the desert rocks. Altogether as healthy and sweet a dead bull as Ben had seen around—he'd tell Sterling that.

The sun was already gone from the hollow; it was getting late in the day. Ben climbed back up the hill to his fire. Now he was glad he'd built it so big—it was still coaling. He stuffed a chunk of saddle blanket down his split boot. Then he cut off a couple of leather saddle strings, dug some holes in his boot leathers, and produced a kind of make-do lace.

When he left her she was still lying there. But she was breathing, he could see her breathing. He wondered—if she staggered up after a while, would she go right back to her meal? He guessed she would.

It was night before he was halfway home. But it seemed light as day, with the moon lighting up the snow for miles around. And the workhorses marked a trail straight for the barnyard.

It was a fine night. When he rode into the barnyard himself, he felt good, even if he was tired and his feet were cold. He knew there were feet there but they didn't have enough feeling in them to seem to belong to anyone. Yet they carried him all right when he got down. Of the six workhorses he only needed two, and he thought this as good a time as any to kick the other four out on the meadow.

Three of them he managed to let out a gate. But the fourth one stuck with the two he wanted. So he thought he'd just throw a rope on him and lead him out.

The big gentle horse, surprised by the rope in the night, raised up against the moon, striking. Then happened what sometimes does in the moonlight, a weird confusion of distances, and they were right at one another when it seemed they had been a rope's length separate. Ben threw his arms up in front of his face and his right arm was instantly slapped back down along his side. Then the horse led off quietly and he turned him loose and threw them all some hay.

He kept thinking about it. He tried to make himself know that death had maybe just brushed him by. That he just missed inches of being struck on the skull by a gentle fifteen-hundred-pound horse pawing out at blank air. But he couldn't make it real. Sure, no death makes sense but some are a good deal more fitting than others, somehow, or to someone. And some were nonsense, nonsense, and he thought of Judy again—a girl with a fever and then a tiny sucked-out smell, like a room after a party; that one had never made the least bit of sense or dislodged from his mind in thirty years. So that to this day he could easier stand in a gale than a certain kind of airless room. Something he hadn't made sense of in all that time and believed now he never would or could, for there was none in it.

When he was thawed out again by the stove, he started thinking of Marian—suddenly, as if he'd just recalled who he was and that he had a wife up by town.

For some reason he remembered a night not too long after they were married and just after they'd come here and he'd started trying to farm again. He'd promised her for a couple of weeks or more to take her to Reno and she could pick out some furniture. But he was always busy with something and kept putting it off. Until this one night after they had gone to bed she started getting onto him over it, lying with her back to him and talking about how long he'd put her off and how many promises he'd broken and how if he hadn't intended to do it he shouldn't have ever said he would and on and on. He hadn't said anything in return and was feeling quite chilled by it, until he laid his hand up against her back and knew from the feel of it that what she was doing was all fakery—her tone, and her having her back turned to him talking, even if she did mean what she said. And when he ran the back of his hand on down her back and around between her legs, she broke down completely, laughing, and swore at him because she did break down and laughed and swore again.

He dragged his bed into the kitchen tonight and built the stove up one last time. He didn't feel very lonely. He was terribly tired. He dreamed of oranges. On the sideboard Marian had filled a bowl full of oranges. He opened a cupboard that should probably have had clothes or canned goods in it, and it was full of oranges too, all in a loose pile, tight-skinned oranges of all sizes, still striped green around their stems.

III

From the very beginning he suspected that this wasn't just an early snow but winter. The sky held bright and clear. There was no sign of thaw. At night it was cold enough that in the morning it took a good jab with a pointed shovel to even crack the trough ice. From the meadow you could look up any time and see more cattle trickling down to the feed ground from the surrounding hills.

Ben just about knew what would happen. As soon as Sterling decided too that this was the start of an early winter and not an early snow only, then he'd send Wesley down in a sled to pick him up. With Wesley, who was young, Sterling would send some poor fellow or other, old or young, fated to spend the winter down here alone, forking hay and reading through the pile of old ranch romances and catalogs, poking wood into the stove and trying to find a radio station that would come in, anything to listen to besides the sound of the generator and snow falling. Ben and Wesley would see to getting the calves weaned and started on feed, eating grain and away from their mothers, and would show the new man what to do. Then they'd go on in the sled back, with his mare tied on behind trying to trot with her feet in a runner track like a rope walker, or maybe pulling the sled herself.

He took the battery out of his Diamond-T. Here the truck was going to sit until spring came, or more likely summer. He cursed his luck for that: hauling was their grocery money all winter. But for just a minute or two, before he thought it out, he was almost glad. Sometimes he imagined he'd rather starve in the house warm than get out again and wrestle those truck chains among the icicles or spill cows up and down those slick ramps or wade around in the slogs of icy black holes that the farmyards got to be every winter.

But starving was a bad joke. He'd need a little money, and he didn't know anyone dumb enough to hire him to sit by the fire, though that was the job he preferred. When he thought about it seriously he knew that more than likely he'd end up leasing another truck, or maybe he could shame Sterling out of his for a while. He'd keep hauling and so keep the trade he'd built up. But even if he didn't he could bet that whatever else he might find to do wouldn't be any warmer.

For a couple of days, every time he looked at his snowbound truck, these things ran around in his head past what they were worth. Well, this wasn't a place to make your mind operate. There was no one to talk to, and after a while even thinking seemed a waste of time. Within only a couple of days he'd begun talking to himself out loud and to the team and the mare and the cattle, which amounted to the same thing. If he hadn't gone through the same thing times before, he would have worried about himself.

To pitch hay to that many cattle took him five hours, cold dull ones, and that each day. In the afternoons he saddled his mare and rode back over the feed grounds, doctoring sick calves when he saw them and studying the cows so that he could recognize the sick ones and doctor them later, when he had help.

There were lots of cattle on the meadow now, and in the afternoons they sometimes spread out considerably from where he'd fed them, so that they might be anywhere on the meadow, which was a big one. He rode the meadow slowly, probably not seeing all the cattle on any one day, but really looking at every cow he saw and thinking about her. This went on routinely for three or four days, which might as well have been years, and then he began having troubles, which afterward went from bad to worse.

There were bridges on the meadow and any time you rode across it you had to cross one or two—little rough cedar bridges that spanned the canal. The canal wound around all over the meadow, so that you were surprised to finally figure out it was only one canal and that it must flow downhill from one place to another like any other. In the spring it helped to slowly dry the bog, the canal did, and in summer you could maneuver the big canvas dams across it and shoot water back out across the grass.

The snow itself, except for being clumsy and inconvenient, wasn't bad to catch and doctor cattle in. The footing was all right. But the bridges were icy. In a roundabout way that was where his troubles began. He'd come across a cow with a horn that had grown in a half-circle and the point of it was starting back into her skull. If he drove her up to the barn he could trap her in a chute and saw it off. He had to make her cross one bridge. She wouldn't set foot on it so he roped her and started to drag her across. But the mare's feet got to spinning on the icy boards and he had to turn the cow loose with his rope to keep from going down. That was all right: he could catch her another time and he had plenty of ropes. He decided to take the mare back to the barn and sharp-shoe her with calks before he did anything else.

This was on the fourth afternoon. It was clouding up again and so seemed colder, though it probably wasn't. He found the calked shoes hanging in the barn; they were just about her size, too. He got doubled up under her and went to work. Cold as it was, he poured off sweat for the biggest part of an hour. Before he was done he could look out through the cracks of the barn siding and see it snowing again. All the time—while he pulled the old shoes off and leveled her feet and nailed and clinched the calked shoes on—he talked to the mare: "Okay, mother, that's all right, let me see your other foot now . . . give it to me . . . here, stand up now, don't lay on me or I'll flog your old noggin for you. . . . That's a good little dear—now see if you can keep yourself right side up next time you go ice-skating," and so on.

It was the first horse he'd shod himself for some years. Ordinarily he got Wesley or someone to do it for him. Yet he got doubled up

under her and was able to get the new iron nailed on all right—
pretty well, really, he thought, not badly done. But then when he
straightened clear up from the last foot he felt rotten. And from that
time on, from the moment he straightened up after shoeing the mare,
he imagined his stomach took to him harder and more often than
it ever had. Of course he knew as well as anyone that if that hadn't
started it something else would have. But from that time on he began to wish he was somewhere else, not down here alone.

Even before that, too, he had begun to indulge himself in not eating—with no one around to prod him or cook for him—though he
should have known better. It snowed most of the night. In the morning he stood on the porch again and got ready to go feed. While he
pulled on his gloves and the furred cap and wound the muffler slowly
around his neck, he looked out at the meadow.

This time, when he stepped off the porch, he sank to his knees. He
felt out his own previous tracks, then he only had to deal with last
night's snow. Later on, when he got the team harnessed and went
out on the meadow with the sled, he'd try to drive over the old sled
tracks too, so that the horses would have the best possible go at it.
But that wouldn't be so easy. Beyond the barnyard was nothing to go
by but a few fence lines in the distance, the curving willow-lined
canal, and the lay of the big haystacks. He knew already how the
team would keep sliding off the buried invisible bands of packed
snow and feeling their way back on.

When he reached the barn he saw that the first magpie had been
joined by another, exactly like itself. He guessed it snowed magpies
here, one per storm. Now when he saw there were two he gave up
furiously on magpies and spit on the ground.

The fork was in the sled. Ben harnessed the team and drove out
across the meadow to the first haystack, where he stopped by the
stackyard gate.

The gate was made of barbed wire and upright sticks; this kind of
weather drew it up tight. He had built hundreds of them and opened
thousands. What they called them back home he couldn't remember, but down in most of California they called them Portagee gates
and way out here they called them Indian gates. Sterling liked to say

that it takes five minutes to build one and half an hour to open it.

Before he put his shoulder to the gate Ben brushed a little peak of snow off the vertical so it wouldn't be falling down his neck. When he pressed the upright hard with his shoulder the top wire popped, *twang,* like a banjo string. "Well you don't know your own strength yet, old son," he said out loud, bad-naturedly—sarcastically.

Cattle were all around him waiting. More were coming; they bucked clumsily in the deep snow, cold and feeling fine. He shut them out of the stackyard. Then he proceeded to load.

For every forkful of loose hay in the stack there's a kind of natural pry point, the key he called it, and if you don't find it you're setting your back against the whole great tangled stack itself. Since he'd been, say, fifteen years old, he'd been feeling his way to it gently, and it felt good to find it even now. But even so, when he came away neatly with this first big forkful, and got his hip under it and pitched it on into the sled, there was a sudden grabbing pain. It didn't hurt as much as it worried him, because he didn't think there was a way around it. And it was there again, each time, a point of strain at the inert start of the swing, just as the hay came free of the stack, just at the unavoidable dead beginning of the arc. There was no way around it. He felt as if his key had been found too.

After he loaded the sled he drove back to the stackyard gate and opened it and drove through it, hollering hungry cattle out of his way all the time, and got out again and closed it and got in again and started his team off across the new snow, trying to divine his old tracks. Then he got into the back of the sled and forked off hay as they went, clucking to the horses all the time, for they were tentative today and would have liked to stop at every step. He fanned the hay off across the field. The cows lined up over it. And then back to the stackyard. Three trips from this stackyard and three each from two others: nine loads of hay forked onto the sled and forked off, spread across the meadow. Then he was done with it, early in the afternoon, and he drove back to the barn and put up his horses and went back to the house and the fire.

Later in the afternoon he rode through the cattle. Most of them were lying down now, kept warm by their own full-bellied ruminations, chewing their cuds, lying along the fouled feed grounds among a scattering of hay stems.

He noticed a heifer calf standing by her mother, who was down resting. The calf was standing a little too squarely on her legs, with her head thrust out, looking altogether a little sad. She was a big calf, an excellent deep-hearted full-flanked calf and glowing. She glowed even through her long hair: so she wasn't sick, at least not yet, but only hurting.

When he got around on the other side of her, Ben saw what was wrong. She was blinking a swollen eye. Underneath it, the thick curly white hair of her face was stained and twisted into wisps, stained yellow all below the weeping eye.

She wasn't the first calf he'd seen like that this week. The others he'd caught and doctored. Like the others she'd probably rooted around in this meadow hay with her whole head, caught a seed of bronco grass on an eyelash, and blinked it right onto the surface of the eye. From there it had worked its way under the lid. Eventually the seed might get dissolved by the eye fluids themselves, but by that time she'd be blind in that eye and have an iris white as a pearl.

This was the biggest of the lot. He thought that if a man could raise a whole pasture full of calves like this one and peddle them each fall, then he could soon kiss the bank and its seven percent goodbye and be working on his own money and land—farting in silk. So when the mother cow got up to her feet, he looked her over. She wasn't a big, high-priced, breedy-looking cow but just a common spindly-assed little cow, with a pretty head and what he liked to call a motherly eye. He tried, as he'd done for most of his life, to get one more clue about why one cow will raise a calf like that every year and another cow who looks as if by the book she should, won't.

Anyway that was a dead dream. Snow would burn before he'd make money. Besides that, he wasn't all that interested any more. He wondered why those old habits of thought wouldn't leave him alone, but seemed to flow on as long as blood would.

He had all the room in the world to catch her. He didn't try to catch her right away but let the mare chase her awhile, to take some of the sap out of her, because he didn't want to take her on fresh the way she was—as big as she was and full of wild grass and milk. So he let her run herself down, and then he roped her. When she hit the end of it she bawled, and when she bawled her mother bawled too and started trotting toward them, bawling anxiously.

The heifer did no battle, just lay back against the rope strangling. She had her legs spread and braced and wouldn't fall. He couldn't throw her. He had her front leg in his hands, shoving it against her, locked in joint and square, so that it made a good pry pole. Ben strained with his old thin legs and back and belly against the pure sagging spraddle-legged inertia of her, but he couldn't tip her over. The mother cow came up behind him. She snuffled and snorted and he felt her breath blowing against him right through his hip pocket. He snorted back at her and she jumped away and in her excitement jumped against the rope which in turn slapped the old mare alongside the neck like a rubber band. When the mare jumped the calf was jerked into motion and he pulled the leg to him and then shoved it back at her hard and she went down.

With his knee on her shoulder and her forefoot doubled up in his hands he held her flat. After she quit thrashing he took the short rope from his belt, eased her hind legs across the front one, and tied her down. Her good eye looked up at him, bulging so that he could have flicked it off with his fingernail. He paddled more snow back to the mare and led her ahead so he could loosen the rope and take it off the heifer's neck before she choked entirely. All the time the old cow danced around moaning.

The cow didn't frighten him. He didn't know why. There wasn't a mean bone in her body but that was no good reason not to be afraid of her. Once out of sheer nervousness and in the same circumstance a black cow had bowled him over. And he really had no way of knowing that this one wouldn't. He rolled the heifer over so that her bad eye was up and squatted down over her. The cow was all around him. She snorted and blew little beads of water on his elbow. Her hot, grassy breath, smelling truly like fermented grass, blew on the back of his neck and fanned both his cheeks. She was really beside herself. But she didn't bother him.

It was nothing but the feathery seed of a bronco grass, but it was something the way it hid itself, burrowing down into the corner of the socket. Because even when he peeled back the two lids as far as possible between his thumb and forefinger, all the hidden surface of the candy-striped eyewhite had seemed to be revealed, but nothing else. Until he spread the lids more forcibly at the very corner, the inside corner of the socket. Even then he could finally see just the tiny tail, a few filaments. These he caught between his nails—drew out the seed and flicked it away. She rolled her sweet, stupid brown eye around a time or two and then let it settle back to center, where it could look out at him and mother and the world again.

Whatever it was started before he even got back on the mare. He figured he'd borne up under so much pain in the last fifteen or so years that changes in it frightened him more than they actually hurt him. As if he was his own wife worrying. Anyway now he knew he wasn't going to have to ride anywhere more today but back to the barn.

He rode as though he had a board stuffed down his shirt back, but in spite of that listing and out of time, unable even to keep up with the easy familiar swaying motion of the mare walking.

When he got to the barn and unsaddled, instead of throwing his saddle up on the wooden rack the way he always did, the way anyone would, he found himself just shoving it through the tack-room door. He left it on the floor mashing its own skirts. When he looked at it he was surprised that he'd done that.

He unbridled the mare, turned her loose, and began walking one step at a time to the house. It wasn't hard: he seemed weightless. Yet he wasn't really sure he'd make it: as if he was a wind-up toy that might peter out any time. When he opened the house door he noticed that he hadn't left the bridle in the barn: it was swinging from his forearm. He chucked it in the corner. Blood in his mouth ran up against the back of his gums and across against the underpinning of his tongue. He spit in the sizzling stove.

Wood enough was piled in the two crates by his chair to feed the stove for several hours. (More was on the porch.) Good. He didn't want to move. The last thing he wanted was to have to get up for a while. He didn't want to lie down. He didn't even want to take his boots off right yet. He was weak as a cat. He liked what the wood fire did to his tingling limbs and face. He shed his coat and his muffler and cap onto the floor. There was no way he could go fork hay off that cold sled tomorrow morning, no way, and that was fine with him.

IV

The next afternoon, when Wesley came, Ben was still sitting there. Through the kitchen window he saw the sled come over the rim and start down the sidehill.

A couple of minutes later he saw the horse's head reappear just outside the window, not fifty feet from him. He saw it—the head of the sorrel horse bowed into the bridle, pushing at it, face rubbed afoam by the bridle leather, the tongue of the downsliding sled shoving the horse along and Wesley's hands set against it, hauling back on the reins, so that the horse was all bunched together in a ball, curled and glistening like a red shrimp. Wesley reminded him a little of Popeye. His forearms were solid as logs. Above his heavy jaw the near cheek pooched out, disfigured by a plug of tobacco. He was wearing his mud-colored hat. Another bundled-up capped figure sat beside him on the sled, showing a good crop of gray whiskers. Ben saw it all, just as he knew he would see it—which was strange because how would he know what he would see?

He was half out of his head, Ben was. But he saw it all, whiskers and all. That other figure was the new chore man. It wasn't his wife. No, but the new man without a doubt. The new man whiskers and all. And what business had he looking for his wife? How could he think, why had he thought, that it might be his wife? And wouldn't he have been furious at her for coming way down here? Say, wouldn't he! He'd have read her a good one—or better yet, he wouldn't have spoken.

He imagined Wesley's perplexity and delighted in it. He imagined it to its finest details and delighted in all of them. He saw through Wesley's eyes. So certain he was of everything. Coming over the ridge Wesley first sees *the smoke coming out the stove chimney.*

Fine, Wesley thinks, *everything as it should be.* (If he'd had any doubts before that, it was because a few cows could be heard bawling hungrily even from the ridgetop. Maybe that would bother him, but he'd hardly be aware of it himself, and then he'd see the smoke and be relieved, and hardly know that either.)

Then as he dips down past the house (he can't see into the half dark kitchen, though he tries) and goes on to the barn, he see *them lined up at the fence, stretching out their necks, more and more of them bawling with excitement at the sight of a sled, though it hasn't got hay in it.*

Now Wesley is puzzled. He is on the watch for signs now. A blind man couldn't miss some of them. When he gets up to the barn to unharness, *the hungry workhorses and the saddle mare like to paw the mangers down at the sight of him. The tack room is open to the weather.* He steps inside to hang up the harness. *Ben's saddle is all in a crush on the floor.*

Ben saw all this paced out in time, so that he knew, or at least thought he knew, just the moment when Wesley hung the harness up and saw the saddle. Wesley tells the new man to put up the horse and feed all the animals in the barn. Himself he hurries toward the house. Wesley hurries along in Ben's own tracks, almost running. The tracks satisfy him that Ben is in the house. What is that sort of lizard-trail ripple in the snow, alongside the boot tracks? (that had been made by the bridle reins that dragged all that way. Ben remembered that the ends of them had been snow-wet when he got to the house; but Wesley would never figure that out).

Ben saw it all. Otherwise he hasn't a clear or even a sensible thought in his head. He is occupied by a perverse, mistaken glee. Mistaken, because he keeps imagining how surprised Wesley is going to be—Wesley who expects to find a man very sick, if not crippled, burned, or God knows what. Instead Wesley is going to find him, Ben, taking his ease, sitting with his boots on, his feet up on the stove, keeping warm and—well just sitting like any keeping-warm man.

At the right instant Wesley did come in, fast, betraying himself, banging the door, just as Ben knew he would. But what Ben became aware of really when he looked at Wesley's face was his own appearance. All the heat he possessed had seemed to gather suddenly—or rather he suddenly became aware that it was so gathered—at two places: the high points of his cheeks and in his eyes. Otherwise he was cold and felt himself drained of color. His hair was matted on his scalp. A parade of cold sweat, large drops sticky as sap, lined the lowest furrow of his forehead. He was unshaven, he was tangled, he was pale, his teeth even were out. All that he read in Wesley's eyes and for just a moment reawakened to the real world, but only for a moment and then was as quickly off again into something else.

Without saying hello or anything else he said: "What kind of man did Sterling find to sit down here and chuck hay to his cows all winter?"

Wesley simply looked at him.

"What?" Ben said.

"You look wrung out. What happened? You look like you've been sitting right there since the world began. What's wrong with you? Can you get around?"

With a belligerence Wesley had never noticed before in him or even imagined, Ben said: "Pull that sled up to the kitchen door and point it to town and we'll find out if I can get around," and then shifted as quickly and said "No, my legs are all right in themselves only they won't hold up the rest of me, son. Just hand me my hat and we'll head back on up the country. How's the weather to home, anyway? Ain't this a bitch!"

"Sure," Wesley said.

The new man, who was a stranger, came in and pulled off his cap and gloves. He was a used-up-looking man, as glum and purposeless-looking as old Shorty before him. Ben glared at him as if he was all his enemies rolled into one.

"Look, do you know what's wrong with you?" Wesley asked Ben.

"Wrong? I feel pretty uneven. That's what's wrong. Anyone can tell that by looking at me. Can't they?" Ben kept looking at the new man. "Can't they? How about you? Do you like the way I look?"

The new man wore cast-off britches four sizes too big for him. He had more stubble than Ben had and from the looks of him it was more habitual. He just glowered back at Ben fearlessly.

"How about you?" Ben asked him. "You're not one to say, are you! Careful who you try too far, partner! You'll get in over your head, and for you that's not far—deep, I mean, deep, deep." Then Ben turned to Wesley and said nastily: "Well didn't Sterling find a man to chuck hay to his cows?"

"John Rhodes, this is Ben Webber," Wesley said.

"Yes!" said Ben loudly, punctuating his own name.

"What is he, drunk or just tailing off of one?" asked John Rhodes.

"Now that's stupid of you to say," said Ben coolly. Of course it was true that when he was drinking he used to act a lot the way he was acting now, and the remark actually seemed to pacify him.

"Well boys, there's a lot of cows to feed before dark," he said, "and I'm a little late getting my feet under me this morning." Saying this he stood up with his fingertips on the stove and sat back down again. "You boys feed them; I'll tend the soup."

"No morning, it's suppertime where I come from," said Rhodes, an evidently humorless man.

"Is that true?" said Ben. "If I'd known it was you coming I'd have shaved. For supper too. Maybe you should have phoned."

"You keep your loonies a long way from town," Rhodes said to Wesley.

Once Wesley decided to take Ben back it was the sooner the better. But he had Rhodes to worry about too. He might not take to spending his first evening at the swamp feeding eight hundred cattle alone by lantern light. Not that Wesley cared if he took to it or not, but he might sull up and want to go in the sled back, or who knows what. So Wesley went feeding.

When he did get the sled pulled up by the kitchen door it was way after dark. He told Rhodes he'd be back in a day or two to wean calves.

The night was a clear one. A waning moon had risen. Ben, stretched out on his back, was swaddled in blankets and packed in meadow hay. The last thing Wesley did was load some rocks that he'd heated and wrapped in burlap sacks. He stashed them all around Ben's legs and thighs. Like an admiring child, Ben watched Wesley load the stones. "Aren't those heavy?" he asked.

"It won't hurt the fat bitch to pull a few rocks," Wesley said, misunderstanding. That was when Ben noticed his own mare harnessed and hitched.

"If they're still warm when we hit the ridge over Goose Lake, they'll feel fine," Ben said.

"I don't imagine they'll make it quite that far," Wesley said, "but you're pretty well wrapped up out of the weather."

"I'll say I am." In fact never had he felt safer or warmer, more helpless or better cared for. At the same time, predictable and unpleasant thoughts contrasted his mood directly, if such a thing is possible. These thoughts seemed to surround him, not touching him but floating by persistently, at a distance.

Here he was, wrapped up so and flat on his back. If he hadn't the energy to mind it now, he at least knew he was going to mind it later. He was afraid they could do what they wanted to him now. Flat on his back to their ministrations, their overkind concern—doctors, neighbors, his brother. He could see it coming.

That, and he had been hired to do a job of work he couldn't get done. (Sterling had made a mistake.) He wished he had made a mismove, had had a stroke of bad luck or committed a piece of stupidity—got injured somehow, or taken sick for no reason. Those things could happen to anyone and everyone knew it. But no, his old motor appeared to have just strained and run down bit by bit. That's how they'd treat it. That's the way he felt about it himself, nearly forgetting about his stomach now and the blood he spat. That's how they'd treat it, though they'd never say.

Before Sterling, who he was costing money, he'd have to be apologetic and grateful. And if he refused to act that way, well, it amounted to the same thing. He was costing Wesley his sleep. He'd gone out of his mind. He'd acted the fool before Wesley and a stranger too. Even now, when he spoke he was so naive-seeming and mellow that Wesley must wonder. These things he thought of for a while, but was soon lulled by the wide, indifferent night. He wished it to go on, the night—afraid of his own chair in his own front

room, where they were going to poke and pull him. At the same time
he really wanted nothing so much as to get home. . . .

In his sleep he began to ride inclined, gravitating toward the back
of the sled. His legs instinctively stiffened, and that woke him. It was
darker than it had been. Or so it seemed. He saw where the moon
had set, leaving a little glow on the mountain. But the stars had
grown pale: it couldn't be long till daylight. He had certainly been
sleeping. He was warm. His feet braced themselves against the heel
of the sled. The sled runners whispered; the mare breathed heavily.
By that hard breathing and the incline of his body he recognized that
they were climbing up the ridge over Goose Lake. In a couple more
hours they'd be back to the pavement, where the snowplows ran and
where Wesley had a truck parked.

Halfway up the ridge Wesley let the mare turn crossways to the
slope and get her air. "How are you making it?" Ben asked.

"Not bad, but I've been warmer," Wesley said. "How about yourself?"

"Oh, just right," Ben said.

At the top Wesley let her stop and blow again. Ben raised up a little and looked around once. Now it was coming dawn: no true colors
yet anywhere. The snow wasn't white any more and the sky wasn't
blue. Neither dark nor light. The last stars flickered weakly like bad
low-voltage connections. The lake looked fleshy as a new leaf and as
little like water. As the sled once more broke into motion he fell back
to sleep like a baby and didn't move until they rattled over the railroad tracks that ran parallel to the highway.

The Old Flame

She'd been in low spirits and I gave her a lot of advice on how to raise them. Didn't help, but she got better. No reason why she shouldn't—nothing wrong with her but some broken ribs, and they'd healed. I remember thinking at the time that she wouldn't learn a damn thing from the accident, and that that was a pity. I couldn't decide whether I thought a harder knock would have done her any more good. The one she got seemed hard enough when it happened.

Just when she'd started feeling fairly good again, a man came along who she hadn't seen for years.

Nice-looking fellow, even yet. Lives way off in some little Nevada town she exiled him to, years back. Had to come this way on business—that's what he said in the note he wrote her.

When Margaret told me Toni'd got the letter, I said: "Did she mention the man's name?"

"Wendell," Margaret said.

"Wendell?—isn't he the one she bought that old Desert Lass mare from about a century ago?"

"Same one," Margaret said. "She had a romance with him just after her marriage broke up."

"So she tells me one thing and you another."

"Well, they're both true."

"Doesn't surprise me. Lots of buckets dipped in the well since then; wonder she even remembers him."

"It would be a wonder if she didn't. She wants us to have him over here to supper so that she won't have to spend an evening alone with him unless she decides to."

"Doesn't want to see him?"

"She wants to," Margaret said, "if she could do it without his seeing her. She's afraid he'll be struck by the change."

"He'll lie if he is," I said. "He won't turn and run."

Toni came over that night and sat down at the kitchen table with Margaret and me. More color in her cheeks than I'd seen in months and I told her so.

"Old friend of yours coming to town I hear?" She nodded. "How long's it been?"

"Eighteen years," she said, and blushed.

"That's a while. He'll be pleased to see how you've turned out."

"Thanks. He probably won't recognize me."

"I hope he's done as well. Have you heard from him over the years?"

"Not for a long time."

"You're full of curiosity then, I'll bet—only natural."

"A little," she said. She looked down and rubbed the rim of her cup with her thumb and looked up at Margaret. Seemed I was preventing a conversation, so before long I excused myself and carried my coffee into the front room and started looking over my daybook from the auction yard.

I could hear them jabbering but I couldn't make out the words. "Shut that door," I hollered. Someone shut it, and I opened the heater vent beside my chair and heard every word.

" 'I don't want to see you any more,' I was going to tell him," Toni said.

"Over already," I said to myself. "Damn, they work fast!" But it turned out they were talking about a man named Ben and hadn't even arrived at Wendell yet. One thing on her mind and she'll talk about another.

"So after that I couldn't go up to Ben's stables any more and ride his horses. And after about a month of stewing I decided to buy a horse of my own. That's when I met Wendell. I bought Lass from him and took a few horse-training lessons, and I had a real wild affair with him—the first one like that I ever had where there wasn't a lot of dawdling around. A good thing there wasn't because the whole thing only lasted two weeks. He decided to go back to his wife, not because of me but because of the judge. When I met him they were separated, and he said they were going to get a divorce. But when the judge told him how much he'd have to pay, he decided to go back."

"Oh Toni, you don't believe that do you? Still?" I heard Margaret say.

"Well, not that that's why he went back, but I believe the judge had a lot to do with the timing. If the hearing hadn't been right then, he wouldn't have gone back right then. Maybe we'd have run through each other, or who knows what might have happened, I don't know. We were both only twenty-two. Anyway, the way it was it was cut off."

"What attracted you so about him?"

"Well, he was big and tall and strong and handsome—and I'd been sitting in my house for a month. It was lust at first sight."

"At first sight?" Margaret said.

"Well, if it wasn't I wanted it to be. I wanted to have an adventure."

"I don't know about that man Wendell," I said to Margaret later. "Going back to your wife just to keep out of jail—that's a new one."

"That's not all of it," Margaret said.

"I'll bet it isn't," I said, "but it's all I heard because someone closed that heater vent in the kitchen."

"I know they did," she said. "But I'll tell you some of it. His wife wouldn't let him in the house because he'd been with Toni—and he asked Toni to call her and plead his case for him—can you imagine!"

"Did she turn him down?"

"Yes, but it seems to have been just because she didn't know what to say. He took advantage of all her good feelings. He told her she was too big a temptation for him to resist. So she located him a job and loaned him the money to move. I said to Toni that he sounded a little sneaky to me. Maybe I shouldn't have."

"Did he pay back the money?"

"Yes."

"Well, maybe he's all right. He was no more than a kid himself."

When he came to town Toni called me up to say so. I stopped by her barn to meet him, and I don't know if it's to my credit, but the man did make a good first impression on me.

I found them out in the pasture looking at Desert Lass, who had her head down grazing. Wendell was curly-headed and dark-complected. "That's the kind women like all right," I said to myself.

Toni introduced us, and I stood and helped them look at the old mare.

"You know her from way back," I said.

"I'd never have recognized her," he said.

"A colt or two and they get a little dough-bellied," I said.

"Last thing a man would think of when he thought of her was belly," Wendell said. "Moved like a cat."

"A streamlined one will end up more womb-sprung than one who's on the big-bellied side to begin with," I said.

"Stands to reason," he said; "not much room in there for a colt."

"That's right," I said. "Colt has to bang out a nest for himself and the next one will stretch it on out some more."

"Must be so," he said, "from the looks of her."

"Agreeable fellow," I said to myself; "man you can talk to."

"How many's she had, Toni?" he said.

"Six," Toni said.

"My wife had seven, but one died." Toni just looked at him.

"That's too bad," I said. "Where is it you're from, exactly?"

"Gerlach," he said. "Nevada."

"I know the town but I can't place it. Where is that near?"

"Not too near anywhere," he said. "Seventy miles from Fernley."

"Fernley: I've been through there for sure. Fair-sized place, is it?"

"Fernley? About five hundred in the summer. Right on the paved road, sixty miles west of Fallon."

"Fallon: I know that place for a fact. Ate supper there and lost a game of blackjack. Hundred miles east of Reno?"

"That's right. You're up that way again, stop by. All good roads. Dirt from Fernley to Gerlach, but it's good ground and you don't even know you're in a car."

"I will," I said. "Train horses up there, do you?"

"Those boys up there don't care if their horses go crooked or in a straight line, and if they don't I don't."

"I don't blame you a bit," I said.

"I watch over some cattle for a man. Eight hundred mother cows."

"That's a lot. Have some men working under you?"

"No sir," he said. "No help but two dogs."

"Don't see how you do it," I said.

"I can press my wife into service if I have to," he said.

"Press her into service?" Toni said.

"If I have to," he said.

"Been there long?" I said.

"Gerlach? Ever since I left Los Angeles."

"You don't strike me like a Los Angeles man."

"How old's old Lass there, Toni?" he said.

"Twenty-three."

"Five when I left. Maybe I've changed some."

"Must be quite a change," I said, "to go away off to a place like Gerlach from the city."

"I don't live right in downtown Gerlach," he said. "About thirty-five miles out."

"How'd you happen to locate there?"

"This old girl right here saw an ad: 'Cowboy wanted: High desert; School bus service, house, meat and milk furnished (they meant a milk cow); Two hundred dollars a month; Northern Nevada; Apply box xxx Western Livestock Journal.' Remember that?"

"I remember," Toni said. "He wasn't a city person to start with, Murphy. He was pretty much like he is now, come to think of it."

"I believe it," I said, "but they say a person can get spoiled fast, living in town, young country boy especially. Milking that same old cow day in and day out by lantern light might look a little humdrum after your city."

"Jan milks," he said. "My wife."

"How's she getting along?" Toni said.

"Just right," he said. "Looks good, feels good—for a woman

who's shelled out kids like she has and been alive as long, she gets by all right; that's what everyone says that sees her. I don't pay a whole lot of attention myself."

"That's too bad," Toni said. "I'm glad she's well."

"She does all right," Wendell said. "But you, now, you never settled. I thought you might. Once in a while I'd catch a thought floating through that you'd married and settled down—but you never." He turned to me. "Don't you think people ought to settle down, time they're our age? I understand you're a married man."

"Darned right," I said. "I've been telling her so for years. Just like talking to a log."

"It takes one to know one, Murphy—a log I mean," and Toni gave me a little push on the shoulder.

"I hadn't seen her for a long time, but she looks fine," he said. "First thing I said to myself when I saw her: 'She looks fine!' Don't you!" And he put his hand on her shoulder and shook her, and I saw her stiffen.

"Yep, I'd have known her on the street anywhere," he said, and put his hand back by his side.

Wendell went downtown to get a room for the night.

When I came home from the auction yard Toni and Margaret were busy talking in the kitchen. Usually if they're like that and I come in, they'll look at me and start to wink and whistle. But this time soon as Toni saw me she said: "I'm sorry, Murphy, if I'd known what he was like I'd never have imposed him on you and Margaret—or on myself."

"What's he like?" I said. "Seems to be a nice enough fellow from what I saw."

"Uk," she said.

"Oh, you exaggerate—unless he's done something?"

"He hasn't done anything," Toni said.

"He's a good guy," I said to Margaret. "Takes care of eight hundred cows almost by himself."

"He must be all right then," Margaret said.

"Lives up not too far from where I used to," I said.

"He's a jerk, Murphy. He has eight hundred and one cows."

"Eight hundred and a wife and two dogs," I said. "but the cows aren't his, they belong to his boss. Didn't I hear you say he's just like he always was?"

"He sort of is," she said. "It's hard to explain."

"And you used to like him. Have you changed so much?"

"I don't think so. I hope not. He used to be very good-looking, I know I'm not wrong about that."

"Good-looking man right today," I said. "You know, I believe she's still carrying a torch."

"Yeah, fat chance," Toni said. "People don't get stupider, do they? I must have had rocks in my head. Poor Jan!"

"My, my, and I have to feed him supper," Margaret said.

"Oh, he's just an ordinary fellow," I said. "Hasn't as much respect for the sex as Toni would like—but I blame his wife for that."

"What's she supposed to do—punch him in the eye?" Toni said.

He knocked on the door.

"Shall I let him in?" Margaret said.

"Do we have to?" Toni said. "Let's not!" Then darned if she didn't clap her hand over her mouth and start to have a fit of schoolgirl giggling.

"Too bad we don't have any arsenic," Margaret said.

"Phaa!" I whispered. "Now you two behave yourself! Where do you think you're going?" I said to Toni.

"The bathroom."

"Act your age, you!"

"Really, Murphy, I have to stop laughing. I'll be back."

"You're as bad as she is," I said to Margaret. "Get out of the way. I'll let him in. Go cook."

I opened the door. He'd shaved and had his hat in his hands. "Poor guy," I thought. "Come in, come in," I said. "Good to see you so soon again." I shook hands with him. "Come into the kitchen and meet my wife."

"Hello," he said to Margaret. "Smells good. Toni here yet?"

"In the bathroom doing some last-minute landscaping," I said.

"Is she?" he said. "Suits me the way she is. Older than she used to be, but looks fine."

"You bet," I said. "She'll probably ruin it."

I took him into the front room, and pretty soon she came out, which I was glad to see, and offered him and me some of my whiskey. I'm famous for not being much of a drinker, but I took a drink.

He took one too, and his flowed straight to his extremities, if I'm not mistaken. Toni was in and out of the kitchen setting the table, and he couldn't keep his eyes off her. He kept trying to get her to look at him, and she kept trying not to—and I believe she had more success.

When she was in the kitchen I said to him: "I looked at a map a while ago, Wendell, and you know, it wouldn't be a hundred miles from where you live over to where I used to live—if there was a way to get there."

"Where you from?" he said.

"Little town of Wagontire over in Oregon," I said. "Sixty miles north of Likely."

"Uh-huh," he said. "Can't place it. Good smell coming out of there."

"I'll show you on the map," I said. So I brought out a map, though I had a little trouble getting him to look at it. Toni came out of the kitchen and looked over my shoulder.

"Wendell and I were almost neighbors," I said. "Only a hundred miles from my place to his—no roads though—lava rock so thick you can't even ride a horse across. But it's the same country. My old neighbor Sterling Green, he had cattle on both sides." He sat up at the name. "Know him?"

"Know him?—damn him! I work for him."

"Hah!—you see! Margaret, come in here! You women uht—'scuse me" ("attack the man," I started to say) "—and the man works for my neighbor! Here!" And I put out my hand so he had to shake it again.

"Get Murphy another drink," Margaret said.

"Don't pay them any mind, Wendell," I said. "No wonder you take care of eight hundred cows with just a wife and a pair of dogs. He's the shortest-handedest man in the world, that Sterling, damned if he's not!''

Toni went back in the kitchen with Margaret, and I told Wendell a story or two about Sterling. No one could fault me for not being able to talk to a stranger. He didn't have to say a word or even listen.

"That's turned into quite a looking woman, that Toni," he said. "Different from what she was, but they say we most of us change a little. Took me a while to get used to it, but she looks better every time she lifts a leg. It's a wonder no one ever married her."

"She says you're just like you used to be," I said.

"I've had people tell me I haven't changed. One other old girl told me I didn't look a day older than I did twenty years ago. I told her she didn't either, but I lied to her face."

"I don't blame you," I said.

"I never pay them much mind," he said, "but if Toni says I haven't changed, that's good, the way I see it, because she liked me the way I was, and so to reason it on out, that means there's hope."

"Just between you and me, Wendell," I said, "there's no hope. If I understood you correctly, there's not a hope in the world in that direction. For many another man and boy, maybe, but not for you and me."

He'd been watching the kitchen door in case she ran by, but he turned and looked at me as if I'd said something in Greek.

We sat down to eat. Toni told us where to sit, and she put herself across at an angle from Wendell, which with only four of us was as far away as she could get. Still it was close as he'd got so far, so he proceeded to try to talk to her.

"How's business, Toni?" he said. "How're the ponies treating you?"

"Fine," she said.

"You say you had some kind of accident?"

"I'm almost all right now," she said.

"What happened?"

"A horse fell on me."

"Now what'd you go and let him do that for?" Wendell said, and laughed, big old horse laugh.

"By God she's right," I said to myself. "The man is dense, and so was I not to see it."

"I shouldn't have," she said.

"I'll say you shouldn't have. I never taught you to do like that, did I?"

"No," she said. Never cracked a smile. That chilled him a little, but he didn't give it up.

"Training those horses is no business for a woman. Don't see why you don't settle down and keep house."

"She has more than that to keep her from settling down, Wendell. She has oats to sow, so we'd better let her be. Pass Wendell those peas, speaking of oats."

Margaret and Toni both looked at me, and I was a little surprised myself, when I'd heard what I said. But it didn't phase Wendell.

"What kind of horse fell you you?—just to make conversation," he said.

"A quarter-horse stallion, four-year-old," she said.

"Conversation?" I said to myself. "If you want conversation so bad, I can give it to you." "Shouldn't have been left a stallion but he was," I said. "Man that owns him drove all the way to Texas to buy him, but he's a billy goat just the same. I wouldn't breed a mare of mine to him, I'll tell you that, Wendell!"

Wendell turned and nodded at me. Thought he could get around me with a nod. "Never crossed my mind," he said. "How'd he happen to fall over on you?" he said to Toni. "Slip?"

"No," she said, "he—"

"Slip ha!" I said (why should I let her trouble herself to talk?). "He didn't slip, Wendell. I was right there and can vouch for it, you bet he didn't slip!"

"He's really drunk!" Margaret said.

"Phaa—keep quiet," I said. "Pass that meat over to where Wendell can reach it."

"What'd he do?" Wendell said—to me this time—but I wouldn't even look at him.

"Toni," I said, "if you'd shown him that stick before you got on him that day—you know the day I mean—I believe he'd never have done it to you."

"I wish you'd said so at the time."

"I wish it too, sweetheart."

"What stick's that?" Wendell said.

"Wendell," I said, "you ask about that stick, and I'll tell you: it was a green stick, you see, cut from a bush. About yay long." I held up my hands. "At first it was green, but then the sap dried out of it and it shrank about two inches and turned kind of gray—but it was the same stick and the horse knew it.

"Well, when this horse was first brought to her he had no manners at all. Every time he saw something alive he'd try to fornicate with it: he'd get up and walk around on his hind legs and beller— you know how they do, Wendell—and his old neck would swell up like a bullfrog's." Wendell reached up and rubbed his neck, which had swollen and turned pretty red. "That's right," I said. "The horse's manners were right out of Texas. The owner calls him Golden Son of Yellow Moon or something like that, but Toni and I, we always just called him Tex. (Wendell, you just reach over and help yourself.)

"So the first day, soon as he started in to rear and squeal she stepped off and kicked him in the belly a couple of times and cut that stick from a bush. After that whenever he'd begin to titillate himself she'd pound him on top of the neck, right behind his ears: whack-whack-whack. 'Cut it out, Tex,' she'd say—way you taught her years back, no doubt."

"Darned right," Wendell said.

"Darned right," I said. "That first day it didn't keep him from carrying on, but by the next day he was sore, and by the time two weeks went by she had his attention, and if his mind happened to start to wander she'd just whisper 'Hey now, Tex' in one of his ears. Or if he was sorely tried—say if a mare walked by winking—you know how they'll do, Wendell—with her tail in the air and maybe pissing a little—why Toni'd just hold the stick up where he could see it with his big right eye."

"Murphy—eat your supper," Margaret said.

"I don't mind," Toni said.

"This will interest Wendell," I said. "She'd hold it up where he could see it and he'd subdue his old gonads.

"She rode him about six weeks—that was last winter. Then they took him home to breed a few mares with and didn't bring him back till August. And before she got on him that first time again, she found that same little old stick thrown back in a corner of the tack room. Turned gray, but that horse recognized it, you bet he did, been better if he hadn't. But at first she didn't show it to him, just clambered up in the saddle with the stick stuck in her belt, that's the pity of it. Because if he'd had a chance to carry that stick along in his mind's eye, there'd never have been any trouble, that's what I think—maybe a little pawing and squealing, but no trouble.

"He had a good picture of that stick registered in his brain and he hadn't forgotten what it was used for—but the memory had slipped way back down into his subconscious—that's the way I see it. Wasn't the smartest horse in the world anyway, and darned foolish at times—led astray by his feelings like more beasts than one since the world began—"

"Eat," Margaret said.

"But I'd hesitate to say to a man that he was outright stupid—just thickheaded. Well, we rode along—came to where there were some mares loose in a field. He looked over the fence at them and must have gone to thinking about the good old days back home, tossed his head and puffed his neck up and nickered at those mares. Rattled your jaw, didn't it Toni?"

"I don't remember."

"That's right: I forgot, she doesn't remember a thing. Anyhow, it had slipped Tex's mind that there's a time and place for everything and that there's such a thing in the world as a stick. And to jog his memory she said, 'Tex, cut it out,' took the stick out from her belt, and held it up as of old. He saw it, and it all came back to him, too much all of a sudden, and he threw himself over backwards— landed flat bang on his right side and right on top of her. Darned if I ever saw anything quite like it, Wendell. Looked like he'd been electrocuted."

"And you don't remember a thing?" Wendell said.

"No," she said. "I woke up in the hospital."

"That was unforgiving ground, too—sand, but packed down. When Tex got up and ran off she never wiggled. Scared me."

"Aw," Wendell said, "I hate to think of you lying there like that." And he laid his big right arm out on the table like a ham. I don't know if he expected her to reach across and take his hand in hers or butter it or what. "Sorry I ever got you started training those horses," he said. "A woman like you doesn't need to be in a business like that. If I didn't live so far away I'd see to it that you weren't."

"I hope *you're* drunk, too," Margaret said.

"Good thing you live so far away," Toni said. "Just how would you go about seeing to it?" And she laid down her fork and looked him right in the eye.

"Ha! Watch out, Wendell, you hound!" I said to myself. "Wendell—" I said.

"I don't know *how,*" Wendell said, "but I'd stop you training those horses, because it's only right."

"Wendell, my friend," I said, "I don't know how it is in Nevada, but in Pearblossom the cats scratch. If you antagonize them, I mean. Otherwise they won't, I think. So you'll have to bark up another tree, if you can find any."

"I'll make some coffee," Margaret said.

Toni covered her mouth with her napkin.

"I didn't catch all that," Wendell said. "I haven't seen six trees since I left home, but if I said something you folks took offense at, I take it back."

"No, no—no offense, old buddy," I said. I picked his hand up and shook it. "Toni," I said, "Wendell here said he was sorry to think of you lying stretched out like that, and I really thought you were dead for a minute or two there, and it didn't make me feel so very good, I don't know if I ever told you."

She reached across and ruffled my bit of hair.

As soon after supper as she could get away with it—in fact a little sooner—she stood up, looking shamefaced: she was going to leave him with us if she could.

"You going?" Wendell said. (Dumb as he was, he was the first to see it.)

"I'm sorry to run out on you-all," she said. "I'll see you before you leave tomorrow, Wendell. Thank you," she said to us. "I'll do *you* a favor sometime," and she gave me and Margaret a smile, friendly but not cheerful.

"I'll give you a ride," Wendell said.

"Thanks, my car's here."

"No need at all for you to run off, Wendell," I said. "It's early. Sit right down there and I'll fix you what you've never had."

"Murphy, it's been good talking to you," he said. "You too, Mrs. Jones. Thanks for the supper."

"Goodbye," Margaret said.

"You're welcome, Wendell," I said, "but I wish you'd stay a few minutes longer."

"Can't," he said. "Where's my hat?"

"Nice to run into a fellow from up there," I said. "You take care of that good wife of yours. Tell Sterling you saw me, and if he doesn't say anything too bad about me give him my best regards. When you planning to go back?"

He winked at me. "I'm supposed to head on back tomorrow, but with luck I might stay around a day or two and see the sights."

Toni was behind him with her hand on the doorknob. She shook her head no and made a face.

"Well, then, with luck we'll see you again," I said. "But you never know about that luck stuff: sometimes a man will bow his head and pray for luck and just wind up with a stiff neck." I rubbed my neck, since he seemed to understand sign language best. Then I shook his hand, I hope for the last time.

I saw them out, and when I went into the front room again, Margaret was sitting over by the window, half in the dark, holding a magazine. "Better turn on the light if you want to read," I said.

"Shh," she said.

I walked over and looked out the window. Toni and Wendell were standing by Toni's car. Toni had her hand on the door handle, and he was standing pretty close to her. "Shouldn't eavesdrop," I said to Margaret.

"No," she said. Wendell went to put his arms around Toni, and

Toni backed against her car. "Ouch," she said.

"Those ribs," I whispered.

"You may have to go out and pour water on him," Margaret said.

"Goodnight," Toni said, "I'm going home. I'll see you tomorrow before you leave."

"I feel like that horse that fell on you," he said.

"You sure do," she said. "Look: I don't want to. Can't you understand?"

"Don't want to what?" he said.

"I don't want to do anything but go home and go to bed—all by myself."

"Oh. Why don't you want to?"

"I just don't want to."

"No one will ever know, Toni," he said and pressed himself toward her.

"Will he hurt her?" Margaret said.

"No—he just hasn't got the message yet," I said.

"My God! Not yet!?" she said.

"I don't think so."

"It's just between me and you," Wendell said.

"But *I* don't want to," Toni said.

"Oh . . . you just don't want to?"

"No."

"Oh." He backed up a step and she started to open the car door.

"Toni," he said, "I just want to tell you something."

"What?"

"I'll never forget the first time I saw you."

"That's nice of you," she said. "I won't either."

"You were with Shirley."

"I remember."

"And when the two of you came walking up to the barn where I was working I said to myself: 'Now there's two plums,' and I said to you: 'Anything I can do for you girls?' and you said you were looking for a horse to buy."

"I remember," Toni said. "And I asked you if you happened to know Ben Webber. You were both in the same business, and I couldn't think of anything else to say."

"I don't remember that," he said. "I remember I said, 'Now you girls aren't really looking for a horse, are you? I'll bet you're just out joyriding around.' And you said, 'A little of both.' Or maybe Shirley said that. But I know for sure you were the one that couldn't stand still. You kept wiggling, I remember it because I remember saying to myself, 'Now this one's more of a plum than the other one.' It had to have been you because of what happened after. Because it happened with you, or I wouldn't be here now. And we had a good time, didn't we?"

"Yes," she said.

"But now you say you don't want to, without even a reason."

"No, I don't."

"Maybe it's because of that judge?"

"No, I've no hard feelings."

"That judge was enough to chill a man's ardor. I asked him, 'What if I can't pay that much?' 'Then bring your toothbrush next time,' he said. I'll never forget it. But we had a good time right up to then. When I left I at least had a reason." He put his hand on her shoulder and put his face up close to hers; he didn't seem to want to kiss her but to look in her eyes.

She didn't move a muscle, and he must have read an answer there. (I believe he was a sort of a veterinary psychologist at heart.)

"Then I won't wrestle you for it," he said.

"No, I knew you wouldn't if you ever really understood."

And she said goodnight, got in her car, and drove away.

"What an ordeal!" Margaret said. "I was wrong about his being sneaky."

The Horsebreaker

Some people just get old, but Clyde got old and rich. And he was pretty old, too, before he took it into his head to get rich. Not only that, if he wanted to brag on himself, but he'd gone to a new town and entered a new business to do it. And there was no reason it had to be chalked up to luck, either, unless he wanted to call just being himself lucky. It was no fluke: when he got too old to do anything else, or to feel much like doing anything else, he just naturally began to make money. It seemed to him now that he always half knew that's how it would be.

Even so, there was too little to it. Selling real estate made and kept him rich, but it wasn't really what he did: he didn't really do anything. He was a has-been—and a has-been is better than a never-was, but not much. The stories he told about himself began to ring false even to his own not unsympathetic ear. They were true, those stories: in case anyone doubted it, his brother could always be called in for a verification. But no one seemed to want to call his brother in, nor was his brother very accommodating.

Clyde had an endless number of true and astounding tales to tell about himself: horses and mules he'd broken and shod, miraculous operations he'd performed on the eyes of cows (cutting cancers off them) after the vets had given up; and there were even people, especially in cold weather, willing to sit in his office and listen. There was a big number of stories, but still some were better than others, and Clyde tended to repeat those.

It wasn't senility. For one thing, he wasn't so old, less than sixty;

and as his brother Ben would tell you, he'd always been like that. Only when Clyde called him up one night and announced that he was breaking a horse did Ben begin to wonder about him.

There was not much use arguing with the old fellow, but Ben tried it anyway.

"You say you have a horse you want someone to break?" Ben said. "Talk louder!"

"Try the other ear," Clyde said. (Ben was a little deaf in one ear.)

"What do you want a horse broke for?" Ben said. "You're too lazy to ride one. There's a boy right next door to you who breaks them—at least he has a sign up that says so."

"I know he does," Clyde said. "I don't want one broke—I aim to break one."

"Why mess your nest?" Ben said. "Don't be stunting around—a man of your age. What horse?"

"Little horse belongs to Sterling Green—had his ears stung off."

"Why you know the story on that horse—you're crazier than you act."

"He's never been soft," Clyde said. "Never been properly softened up, that little horse, not till I got ahold of him."

"You'll think soft," Ben said. "I sat in my truck and watched him put two better men than you where it's soft, right in one day."

"I doubt that," Clyde said.

"Doubt it?—doubt what?"

"I doubt two better men. Hey you, don't you remember that pinto mule in Bakersfield? That one who they claimed he—"

"Yes, I have a long memory. I want to talk to you, old son," Ben said.

"How's that skim-milk pig doing?" Clyde said.

"I want to talk horses," Ben said.

"I've got him half soft and soaking tonight. His neck needed pounding. Tomorrow I'll have him in the sack. I'll have him in the sack tomorrow. They don't buck with their head up. You know that. Anybody knows it. What's unknown is how to keep it up. They've got to be soft and you've got to have quick hands. Say, my hands are still fast, you know that? Damn right!"

"You're fast all over," Ben said. "I want to see you in the morning."

"All tied up," Clyde said. "Down to my office at two, be down to my office at two and I'll talk to you then. Squeeze you in. On the instant—whereby all expectorations remaining unramified I'll perpetrate."

"Don't real estate me," Ben said. "You just tell me now that—"

"Hey, let's go to Reno tomorrow night," Clyde said, "what do you say? We'll get this young horsefighter next door to go with us and we'll all get drunk together and puke in each other's hair. He can't do his wife because she's eight months along and out of town. We're sick of this town, all of us. I feel revigorated. How about yourself?"

"I feel as if I shoveled ditch all day on a sour stomach," Ben said. He'd have to try to remember to go to his brother's office the next day at two, and see if he was still alive.

Earlier in the day the young horsefighter next door had lost a fight with a horse, and that was how Clyde got into it.

First of all, weeks ago, he'd seen the boy move in, and he'd gone over and introduced himself. The boy didn't seem big on talking about himself, but that was all right with Clyde. Then from his porch Clyde had off and on watched as the fellow built himself a round corral that could only be a horsebreaking corral. Worked kind of slow but didn't do a half bad job: big juniper posts set *deep* in the ground—judging by the length of time it took him to dig the holes in that easy sandy ground—and then circles of cables in which were inserted a great number of vertical pickets and brushy branches, so that you could hardly even see through it when he was done.

Then he'd hung out a shingle, just a few days ago:

HORSES BROKE, TRAINED AND SHOD
Guaranteed

Clyde figured that the word "guaranteed" gave him away: he wasn't familiar with breaking horses for the public. Most people couldn't stay on top of a sawhorse, and there was no use promising they could.

Then Clyde, sitting by his stove in the morning, had heard a truck gearing down. He went onto the porch and saw Sterling's outfit come by, carrying a lone horse whose head was stuck up as high as possible over the racks, looking out. It was the little horse Sterling called Hornet, who'd been into a bee's nest as a colt and lost the tips of his ears. And Clyde said to himself that wasn't the only story he knew on the horse.

He watched the truck turn into his neighbor's lane and back up to the loading chute. He told his wife to go down to the office and open up; he wouldn't be down. Don't call him unless there was something so live it just couldn't wait. Sterling left, and his wife left, and Clyde wandered around the house. It was midmorning before Wesley finally led the horse out to the wicker corral. None of my business, Clyde thought, but the boy gets to his work kind of late in the day.

Clyde drove over, sneaked up, and peeked through the pickets. It wasn't polite, but what else could he do? The horse was saddled and ready. The horsebreaker was adjusting himself. Clyde counted the times he pulled down his hat and rearranged his chaps. The horse appeared calm, acted gentle to handle, quiet.

Suddenly he wanted to yell through the fence, "Jesus Christ get a short hold on the reins and pull his head around *to* you!" But what did he care? It wasn't him in the corral. The boot went in the stirrup and without so much as an eyeball flicker Hornet jumped ahead and stuck a hind foot in the horsebreaker's belly.

The stirruped boot jammed against the horse's heart; the rest of the horsebreaker's body flew back and his head struck the ground. The horse snorted a little and jumped sideways. The boy was jerked a few inches when the boot came off and hung alone in the stirrup. There it was, stuck, an empty boot, and for the first time the horse seemed really scared. He ran to the fence, hit it, and spun, whistling through his nose and rolling his left eye and all the ears he had toward the boot. With the accuracy of one who had been desperate before, the horse cow-kicked the boot from the stirrup and sent it spinning across the corral. Immediately he subsided and stood where he was.

Clyde looked at the horsebreaker. His hat was off. Stretched out there, he looked still younger. Hardly twenty, and there was a hole in his sock. The horsebreaker had told Clyde his wife would be arriving in a few days, and that she was going to have a baby. Clyde imagined her unable to darn a sock, potbellied and popping with milk, legs like an antelope: delicate! *that* was what he liked. He wondered if they'd been married long enough . . . then he began to wonder if the boy was ever going to get up.

The horsebreaker did sit up then, and began making sure all his parts were operating. Work down from top to bottom, Clyde thought. The best thing for him to do was to sneak away and come back and announce himself. He walked off among the barn and sheds, turned, and slowly came back.

Clyde yelled. The gate rattled and swung. "Good morning," Clyde said. "Or is it still morning? How are you and Bee-ears getting along?"

"I'm not so sure," the horsebreaker said, blinking. "I haven't been on him yet."

"You haven't, huh? Let me put it to you this way," Clyde said. "How much do you know about this horse?"

The horsebreaker was blinking rapidly, then succeeded in stopping. "Sterling said he was well started."

"He told you the truth then," Clyde said. He laughed, eyes aglitter. "He's been started more than any horse around and by more different men. You don't mind if I sit on the fence and watch?"

"Do whatever you want," the horsebreaker said.

"I like to ask. Some don't want anyone around. To tell the truth, I never did myself. I never liked anyone around." Clyde waited for the horsebreaker to draw him out about his past. "When I was breaking horses," he added. At last he broke silence again himself: "Have you rode many colts?"

"My share of saddlebroncs."

"Rodeos," Clyde said. "Ah now, that's another business altogether now isn't it?"

"Whatever you say."

The horsebreaker caught the horse and led him to the middle of the corral. This time he did try to pull the head around, but the

horse's neck was no more pliable than Clyde's stiff old boar's-dick
quirt. You never thought of softening him up a little? Clyde said to
himself.

He started up the fence. He picked the biggest post. When he
grabbed hold of it he felt it was broken off at the bottom, hanging
from the cables now instead of supporting them. Could that horse
have broken it? Surely Wesley must have backed into it with a
pickup. Clyde crawled up the fence and got on top of the post anyway. If they'd gone a little farther out in the hills, he thought, and
cut down a little bigger tree, the post would never have broken,
would have been stronger in the ground and broader on the top and
a little more comfortable sitting.

At least this time the boy was taking a short hold on the reins, and
he kept his back near the horse's front end and got a deathhold on
the horn before he put his foot in the stirrup. When the horse threw
his wingding, the horsebreaker went right on up into the saddle.
Clyde was elated. Of course with the horse's head free, the horsebreaker never got seated, nor even a foot in the right stirrup. Down
again, soft this time, carefully brushing the shit out of his hat.

Clyde could see that Hornet did only what needed to be done. Like
a mule, saving himself. Better and harder things ahead. The boy
would never get settled on him the way he was going at it, that was
plain. It was a disappointment. He would like to see the horsebreaker get a good seat, just once. He wanted to see if the horse
would walk astraddle of his own neck and squeal like a dog, at least
for a jump or two, or throw himself on the ground. No, he doubted
that last. It was a puzzle, curious, the end predictable but not the
action. He himself was shivering; he crossed his arms and wished for
his coat.

Up again, the horsebreaker said, "Hornet, he's further along in
his education than I am."

"Lookit here, son, maybe it's not mine to say," Clyde said, "but if
I was you I believe what I'd do is to—"

The horsebreaker turned on him, cocked his head up to Clyde sitting on the high post like God. "Lookit here yourself. If you were me
and I were you, you'd be down here and I'd be up there, but if I was

you I'd keep more quiet. I've had all the big-hatted advisers I need."

Clyde was calm. "What would you give a man to start this horse?" he said.

"You'd better watch yourself," the horsebreaker said, and turned away.

Face blanched, Clyde stood, boot-balanced on the highest cable, poised like an eagle. He started to jump, cast his weight forward nimbly as any man, one boot heel jamming between two pickets where they met the cable, the rotted-off post lurching, and he swung forcibly like a hinged board, face first.

"Man overboard," the horsebreaker said.

Clyde dragged himself up, red-faced and spitting sand, and turned to inspect the part of his boot heel that remained in the fence. He dug it out with his knife and put it in his pants pocket. "Two dollars to get it fixed back on," he mumbled.

Yet before the horsebreaker was through smiling Clyde pried him again. "What would you give a man to start this horse for you?"

"Why just what I'd give to see a piss-ant eat a bale of hay. All I have. Which is nothing. At least you couldn't further spoil him."

"What's Sterling paying you?" Clyde said. "No, never mind. You feed him and keep him and let me use your place and I'll start him for you. It won't take long. Five dollars a day and you pay me when Sterling pays you."

"Well I'm not your daddy," the horsebreaker said. "You be the fool and I'll be the audience."

Without unsaddling the horse, the horsebreaker climbed onto Clyde's post. Clyde drove home, lifted *his* saddle from a hook in the barn, opened the old war chest: took out his quirt, a snaffle-bit bridle with soft rope reins, a hobble made of a split and twisted tow sack, a soft cotton rope an inch and a half thick, and a lariat a little mashed by storage. He cut the wires from a bale of hay and twisted them into a slender baling-wire bat.

When he faced the horse, he noticed that even the air in the bottom of the corral was considerably different from that on the post. The horse flicked his foot at a fly and Clyde felt a twitch in his own thigh, like the reflex from a blow. When he bent over to sort his equipment his face got red, and when he stood up it got white—he had that kind of face. Too much pork and chair, he thought. For a moment he felt as if he'd gone by a gully with something dead in it. Then he was all right. He felt good. He disregarded his audience.

With one hand he took hold of the rein up close to the bit and with the other threw the cotton rope over the horse's head and tied a knot in it around the base of the neck. He wondered if the horsebreaker had ever seen anyone tie a bowline with one hand. If he had an eye in his head he'd notice. Clyde flicked the slack of the rope between the hind legs. A foot raised to kick was hooked. The horse didn't throw a fit: apparently this had been done before too, and done well enough so that he was afraid to fight it. Clyde drew the leg up high under the belly, twisted the escape out of the rope, and tied it off. He pulled the saddle and bridle from the fouled horse and went to throw them up on the fence, swinging them neatly off his hip. To his surprise the saddle fell back into his arms. It was too high, he couldn't make it. "Here," said the horsebreaker, and in some embarrassment Clyde handed them up.

Clyde changed his rope. For the horse, then, to jump would be to fall. Hornet wouldn't make the move and Clyde couldn't pull down the braced weight. Facing the horse to the fence, Clyde tied the foot ropes forward to a post and suddenly struck the horse in the face with the heel of the quirt. Hornet in terror jumped backwards, hind legs snatched forward, falling. Clyde was fast: jerked the knot loose from the fence and fell on the falling animal's head. He lay down alongside Hornet, one knee plunged against throat, other knee hooked around muzzle, locked his legs together and twisted the head as hard as he could. He reached up and tightened the leg ropes with his hands.

He was a little surprised the horse didn't thrash his head, even when it was released, or strain against the ropes. This had most likely all been done to him before, yet it must have been a while ago. The horse began to sweat. Clyde noticed it first at the flanks—just a dark turn to the hair. Then all the body oozed at once, or so it seemed. There was water in the crease below the chopped ears; it rolled in and out of the eye sockets and trickled from the nostrils.

With the baling-wire bat Clyde struck the supple part of the neck. The horse curled from the ground, face wet and slick, wet ears pinned flat, mouth striking. Clyde mashed his heel into it, stood on the horse's mouth and continued pounding with a rapid stroke.

Noon, and no one to cook. He fried him some sausage. For business purposes he had a sticker on his car: "Eat beef for health." But pork was really his meat and sausage his cut. "I like the grease off the meat," he was fond of saying. After lunch he hated to leave the shade of his porch. Yet at one sharp he was back in the corral. He rolled the horse over and began pounding the other side of the neck. The horse had turned black and settled the dust around him. Apparently there was no end to the water he could put out. The boy was there on the post. Was he there again or there still? Surely *again,* Clyde thought. Who would sit staring at a tied-down horse for an hour, without even a speck of shade? With veterinary curiosity Clyde reached between the hind legs and stroked the hairless chocolate-colored skin where the testicles had been cut out three or four years ago.

The horse needed hind shoes. Clyde hated the thought. Yet now while he had him down was the time. Rather than build a fire and shape some shoes to fit properly, he drove down to the hardware and bought some pre-shaped and -sized "cowboy" shoes. He asked the horsebreaker to lend him some tools. They included a pair of fine hand-forged nippers that had been worn out once and repinned. He wondered if the boy didn't shoe horses better than he broke them. It was true that his knuckles were scarred and he had a proper curl to his shoulders.

"Don't you tell anyone who shod this horse," Clyde said. "I guessed his size: he only takes an aught shoe and's got a six-year-old mouth. Nice small feet." Clyde unbent his back and glanced down at his own feet, which were also small (the horsebreaker's weren't), proving that he, Clyde, was a rider, not a plodder.

He clinched the shoes on to stay, if not to fit. It seemed his back would never be half straight again—and here he used to shoe some-

times eight or nine head in a day. An idiot's life! Though maybe he
hadn't thought so then. . . .

Clyde untied the ropes, hit the horse with the sack hobble; Hornet
scrambled up, shook, staggered, planted his feet squarely and stood
blinking. With a rope Clyde jacked up a hind leg as before. He hobbled the front legs together and jumped and struggled onto Hornet's
back. The horse stood a second, then, even fouled as he was, snorted
and erupted, sprang in the air, and fell on his ribs. Clyde was thrown
clear on hands and knees, perfectly clear yet arms and legs churning
like a pig on ice. He got on his feet and whipped the horse up
quickly. When he got on again, Hornet stood. Clyde moved around
over the back, petting and massaging for what seemed endless minutes, but the horse never stopped shaking.

Clyde brushed the horse's back and belly with his hand and saddled him. "Let's tie him in your barn," he said. "When he cools off,
you can feed him and pack him some water."

"I'll take him," the horsebreaker said. "You're not going to unsaddle him?"

"Uh-uh, I want to see what he does. I don't want to tell you your
business, but if you're going to lead him you better get a hold close
to his face."

The horsebreaker opened the gate, holding the exhausted horse
on twelve inches of slack. Hornet bogged his head and took it. Hind
feet crossed the boy's face, hit the brim of his hat.

"I'll get your hat for you," Clyde said. "Rope burn you?"

The horsebreaker flapped his hands and stared fascinated: "Poo-
tah la Maggie, look at him fire."

The horse was mopping the barnyard with his nose on the ground,
breath shooting gravel at their knees. Stiff-kneed landings drove the
stirrups straight in the air where they clashed repeatedly over the
saddle, the stirrup leathers snapping like whips. A fog of dust ob-
scured him and when they saw him again he was running.

"Could you ride your pony if you ever got seated on him?" Clyde
said.

"I don't imagine, but that's for me to ask you."

The horse ran down the lane, slid up to the gate, spun and came galloping back. Clyde stood ready in the end of the lane with a loop hidden behind him. He would have liked to turn him a flip, and as the horse shied by he did forefoot him neatly. But the instant the loop enveloped his legs, Hornet planted himself and slid to a stop. They anchored him for the night.

"You're not going to unsaddle him now?" the horsebreaker said.

Clyde said he wasn't. He drove home, wandered out to find his cow, who was waiting for him near the barn, tight-bagged, and he milked her crudely with stiff fingers.

The evening was unpleasant. His wife didn't like what he was up to and said nothing to him except that he must call Ben. No business would be talked tonight. When he'd finished supper and watched television a bit, he did get up and call. But Ben's words and her silences had equally little effect on Clyde.

The next day the horsebreaker limped out of the barn. "I led him to water and tied him back up," he said.

"Uh-huh. How'd he lead this morning?" Clyde said.

"Sudden."

"Huh. You kept ahold of him though, right? You reached and got him and snatched him back. You're waking up. To tell the truth, I saw you from the porch." Clyde untied the horse and led him to the corral. The neck was swollen, a small ridge on each side, but the real soreness would be underneath, in the muscles. Clyde was satisfied. He thought, Bee-ears, you're tender and bendable as a flower. There were mouth corners yet to be done.

He tied the left rein to a ring in the left saddle skirt and had the horse chasing himself, whirling from the pressure and from him—Clyde—who stood there snapping hobbles and kicking dirt. This was done on the other side too, and the skin where the black lips met was peeled down to pink by the bit rings. Clyde tied long ropes to both bit rings, ran the ropes back through the stirrups, and began driving the horse from behind like a plowman.

He jumped the horse into a trot, stayed well back himself, and made the inside circles. Still he had to open his mouth to get enough air, and what he got seemed straight dust.

"Can you open the gate?" he said. Hornet spurted through the opening. Clyde let him run the length of the lines, threw his weight onto one. He had the leverage. The head whipped around, the body flew on, circling the head, unfooted, helpless, ungainly, crashing. It was a while before Clyde could get the horse up. After that he had him turning every which way and stopping, hooves sliding, making short figure elevens in the gravel. He had a good natural stop, Clyde thought. Wasn't it time to quit? He had almost run out of air himself. And if he went too far the horse would be immune to feeling. Soft and watching—and if he was any judge the horse was at that point. Though you never knew if a little less or a little more would do better. Who could say? He looked at his watch: ten-thirty. He'd rest until one, maybe even go without dinner.

At one Clyde brought back a short leather strap with snaps on each end. With this he hobbled the stirrups together, passing the strap across under the horse's belly.

Holding the reins short, and getting the cheek of the bridle tight in his hand, Clyde pulled the horse's head around and made him whirl in a circle. He was at the center, and he kept the horse spinning even after he was in the saddle, until he had the seat he wanted. The horse was grabbing himself, tail clamped, back humped, trying to buck with his head up. Clyde suddenly drove a spur in him, snatched him to the left again, driving the right spur. Pulled him back and forth then and into the fence, loping finally, Clyde's feet driving him on. The horse had a right to scotch, for every time Clyde suspected him of getting wits and balance together he slid a hand down one rein and pulled the horse hard into the fence.

The head busy, the head busy, Clyde thought, soft as butter. The horse lathered white between the legs and specks of blood showed at the mouth corners. They never slowed up. "Swing the gate once more for me, son, if you would," and out they shot.

Clyde let him run halfway across the barnyard, spurs gigging him on, then he set down so hard on one rein that he was afraid the horse would turn another squawdeedo, this time land on him. Hornet did start to fall sideways, stumbling, and Clyde threw the reins to him, let him gather his feet, and then snatched him again, this time the other side, whirled him both directions and off they went right down the center of the highway, Clyde still jerking the horse in circles first one way then the other and gigging him with both spurs, sparks flying off the asphalt, Hornet given no chance to forget he was being used.

The skidding shod and unshod hooves rang on varying pavement. Their tracks would be there in the tarry patches, Clyde thought. Immortal! Or at least until the first hard freeze this fall. For a minute he was afraid the streets would be deserted. Then he straightened his back in the saddle, swelling like an old boar, the bull of the woods, drawing in his belly, increasing by inches. The horse seemed to dwindle.

A motorcycle passed: Hornet rolled an eye, leaped, was pulled easily around, stumbling. Clyde imagined what they'd say tonight in the Frontier Club. . . .

Someone stepped into the street, hailing him. Clyde said, "Is this the horse you think it is? I expect it is. Only horse around's had both ears stung off. . . ." He went on, stopped again: "Uh-huh, I brought him in right off to get used to the boogers. He's never been uptown before, do you imagine? 'Cept just passing through, trying to stare the slats out of a truck. What do you say?"

Ben was standing in front of the office. Faces of children were pressed to the window of one of Clyde's duplexes across the street. He heard the excited hum of voices coming through the walls, though he finally realized this was a television.

Ben bowed and took off his hat, a wild head of hair springing out like the white beard on a goat.

"Yessir!" Clyde said. "Do you want to talk to me?"

"I did but I don't," Ben said. "I changed my mind. You'd best go on before she decides to come out of the office."

"She won't," Clyde said. Yet she might, and he rode on.

Heading out the other side of town he was light-headed. I should have eaten a little, he thought, a piece of bread and honey or some plum jam by itself. He turned across the canal. When the hooves rattled the bridge boards, Hornet snorted and tried halfheartedly to bolt. Clyde pulled him around. "Ante," he said. "If you've got to be a nigger, be a good one." You're in the sack now, he thought.

They jogged on across the juniper flat, skirting town and heading home. He put his reins in one hand now. Something gray appeared at the edge of vision: "Coyote," Clyde said, and lifted his free hand. Hornet jumped sideways and landed stiff-kneed, an ear cocked at Clyde who'd been snapped off center. A hair off, but Hornet took it. Mouth open, Clyde's teeth smashing tongue, Hornet's head gone out of sight and the noise coming up, like a stuck pig or a dog in the mower blades, continuous.

It was this squealing terrified Clyde. He got his seat back, as good a deep socked-in seat as anyone ever had. Boots jammed to the heels down the hobbled stirrups, spurs jobbed into the cinch and through the cinch to the hide and through the hide, an arch thrown into his back and his weight against the reins trying to control the head, drawing mouth blood too, all he could, though that wouldn't help now.

Clyde grunted. The horse too, whose body couldn't stand its own lock-kneed hitting. Hornet's mouth showering back a bloody salt into Clyde's eyes and he himself spitting air. He refixed the jumping desert each time they landed. Forced himself not to be confused by the sky, to keep refocusing the horse's neck against the ground. His eyes were gauging accurate, but beginning to lag, lagging, falling behind like the bubble on a spinning level. He was being moved, knew he was, crotch drifting, will couldn't stop it. Off center, a hump jerked into his back, the left leg taking too much shock, the right one springing loose, spur popped from the cinch.

He lost the stirrup, felt it go, and only hoped then to lose the left one too. Mane glimpsed against the sky, track all lost of where he was, while he felt it there solid, his foot stirruped, hobbled, spur spurred into the cinch and through it, twisting now like a hook; he the fish now, a whole new set of things to think about, too fast, rising changing sand bushes. Clyde's face passing Hornet's mouth, open, blood on the bit rings, eye glazed visionless. Bucking blind, then quit and ran.

For fifty yards Hornet tried to kick him loose. Clyde dragging. His eye buried in the crook of one arm and the other arm enfolding his head. Even during this he imagined the luck of the foot breaking, getting sluffed out of his boot. The horse hit the badger hole, folded down upon Clyde's leg. He thought this was salvation and spun over onto his back, watched the horse pawing up again, saw himself still hooked, suspended, moving off, face slapped by branches, and discovered his hands lacing around juniper trunk. And him knowing he could pull his leg off if he had to. An explosion in his knee, vision of juniper roots bursting, fibers flayed out like the nerve ends on a lighted chart. The saddle fell on his feet, the horse tangled in bridle reins, stepping on them and brutally stabbing his own mouth. Hornet stopped, tied to his own legs.

Clyde discovered that he was still squeezing his juniper. He let go. Who saw? He turned slowly. She would be there, arms across chest; Ben quizzical, hat off, head at an angle; the boy who wanted to break horses; behind them a great vague crowd of townspeople. No, he saw the buildings of town, that was all, and farther west the ridge of his own canal bank.

He fished up his knife, leaned forward and cut a few strands of cinch away from his spur. If the latigo on the saddle hadn't broken, the strands would have, he thought. He pulled his boot from the stirrup and got up. As far as he could tell, nothing was broken, and neither back nor knee would be impossible until tomorrow. All the rest was skin, the knees and elbows ripped out of his clothes, bruises, teeth. He must have hit his mouth. Where was his hat? There. Way back there. Well, he'd gone a long while with his own teeth, hadn't he? Way longer than Ben.

His inclination was to pull the bridle off Hornet and start walking. But if he left the horse here, this whole story was going to be out an hour after feeding time. And what if he led him in? If he walked alone he could wade the canal anywhere, but the horse wouldn't follow him through the water. He'd have to go to the bridge, which was right by the highway and visible from the horsebreaker's house too. It wouldn't do to be seen leading the horse in, and if he waited till dark, his wife would have the whole town out after him. There was nothing to be done but to mend his latigo and be seen riding in, if he was to be seen at all.

Clyde threw his stirrup hobbles away and hid the spurs in the badger hole. He couldn't control his knee and didn't want to be spurring
the horse by accident. This was one ride he wanted to sneak. He
hobbled Hornet with a rein, saddled him, and when he went to get
on cheeked him tight as the mouth could stand—not much now.

The horse dragged his toes, even over the rattling crossboards of
the bridge. But Clyde wasn't taking any chances: he kept his eyes on
the horse's head. If he'd dared to look around, he might have seen
the listless dragging tracks Hornet was making in the sand, and
been less nervous.

Clyde was a couple of days in the house recuperating, and when he
did go back to the office he looked pretty bunged up. The horse was
loping along like a good one and stuck his foot in a badger hole and
took a tumble: that was the story Clyde thought of telling, but he
was afraid it wouldn't be believed and changed his mind. Besides,
the episode as it really was was good enough.

And it was lucky for him that he didn't try to lie. That darned
Sterling, the first day Clyde was back at the office, knocked on the
door of Clyde's house and asked his wife if it wasn't okay to borrow
something out of the tack room. She told him to go ahead, and under
pretense of borrowing something (though he really did borrow something), he looked at Clyde's saddle and found the track of the right
spur rowel where it had crossed the seat of the saddle on Clyde's way
off—and Sterling told everyone about it.

Ben stopped in at the office a week later, to say the pig he was fattening for Clyde was ready (he also wanted to have a look at him).
Once there, he regretted it, and could hardly wait to make his escape.

"You saw yourself," Clyde said to him, "I had him between my
two hands. Soft as butter, don't you doubt it."

"I don't doubt it," Ben said wearily. "I saw it myself."

"Only I ought to have kept both hands on the reins at all times.
Darned if a man no matter how much he knows and how well he
knows it won't always lose his wherewithal at the sight of a coyote or
some silly thing."

"Now there's a bit of first-class wisdom for you," Ben said.

Clyde was having some teeth made, but right now he was missing some out of his mouth like an old cow. It didn't make him look younger. And he had a new cane—Ben saw it leaned up against the desk—to help him out with his knee. But for all that, he appeared to be in a lively enough mood.

Ben thought he'd bait him a little. "How long again you say you rode that horse?"

"Two days, so far."

"Two. . . . Pay you, did they?"

"Five a saddle."

"Uh-huh—ten dollars. That pay those dentist bills pretty well, will it?"

"I've just about got that dentist sold a piece of property," Clyde said. "Anyway he's easy money from now on, that horse—you could sit on him backwards."

"Not me," said Ben.

The Drowning

That boy Larry who drowned was twenty-eight years old and simple as they come. You had to watch out for him every minute, which we proved that day beyond a doubt.

Simple or not, it was hard to see afterward how he'd managed to drown. The river was low, and he'd crossed it I'd say maybe twenty times—all of them earlier in the summer when the river was higher, and all in the same spot and on the same old reliable horse.

We'd gathered cattle that morning and came to cross the river with them just before noon: two hundred cows with their calves and five of us. Roy, who was the foreman, and Gordon had already crossed and were up on the far bank keeping the cattle bunched as they came out of the water, but staying back quite a ways so as not to impede them.

When the last of the cattle started into the water I climbed down off my horse to loosen my cinch before I crossed. A horse swells up in the water, or when he swims (I don't know if it's the water or the swimming that makes him expand), and if the cinch is tight to start with, then it may bind into him around the heart and lungs hard enough to make him lose consciousness or paralyze him—which doesn't augur well for the person on him, especially if he can't swim.

So I loosened mine. While I was still on the ground I looked under my horse's neck and saw Larry standing beside his horse with his hand under the stirrup leather, messing with his cinch strap. "Good enough," I thought. Also I saw Ben, who was just a few yards the other side of Larry. He'd already been off and loosened his cinch and got back on, and now he was sitting cocked sideways in his saddle, leaning back taking it easy with one hand on his horse's hip, and facing Larry. (I'd noticed earlier that Ben kept an eye on him, even though no one had told him to and even though he'd never seen Larry until that day.)

They say a person shouldn't take anything for granted, but you'll never get anything done if you don't. Even if Ben hadn't been over there, I'd have naturally figured Larry'd remembered to loosen his cinch—since why else would he bother to get off his horse and fiddle with it?

Anyhow, we rode into the water. I can't swim, so I was busy looking at my horse's ears, trying to keep track of my own affairs, when I heard Ben yell (never a peep out of Larry).

I looked around and saw no Larry and no horse, then the horse's legs came up out of the water and he rolled over two or three turns like a barrel, washed over into shallow water, and when his feet struck bottom he floundered and staggered and got up on them and clambered up the far bank shaking his head—just the horse. By then Roy had his boots off and was in the water. He could swim and so could Ben. Gordon and I got in too, and wallowed around as best we could. But he was a hard boy to find when you wanted him, and when Roy pulled him out he was white as a rabbit. We pumped a few cupfuls of water out of him, but that was all—couldn't get him to draw a breath.

It wasn't what we'd had in mind, and no one knew what to say or said much of anything, except to swear some without knowing what at.

There wasn't a dry sock among us. Ben pulled his boots on over his bare feet, which is about the closest thing I've ever seen to a miracle—don't see how he managed it—and went off picking up sticks on the desert. He's a thin, long-legged man, and when he bent over his shirt bagged forward off his shoulders, and with his naked legs stuck in his boots he looked like a chicken scratching. (And he stayed pretty much bent over because that's a juniper desert, covered with trees, and there's sticks all over it.)

The same three or four cows that had spent all morning trying to break away were beelining off now, and some of the rest of the cattle were starting to scatter too, though not in such a hurry. "What do you think?" I said to Roy, who was down on his bare knees blowing on some dead grass he'd lit for tinder underneath the first batch of sticks Ben had brought back.

"We'll have to let them go, Murphy," he said. He said two of us should stay the afternoon with the body while the other two rode back to town after a jeep. Would have been quicker to pack him out directly on a horse, but Roy said he didn't want to take a chance of bruising him up, for the sake of his mother.

So we let the cattle go.

After we'd tried to revive him we'd left him lying there by the river, on the damp ground. Naturally had, without thinking about it. That was a gravel beach, and it hurt our feet even to bear our own weight. But we built the fire on dry ground, up out of the river bed and fifty or sixty feet from the body. We propped our clothes up to dry, and by the time we stood backed up to the fire for a bit, I felt halfway over the surprise or shock of the drowning.

I watched the cattle spread out and drift off. One big calf not far from me was standing under a juniper tree bawling for his mother, who he'd got separated from crossing the river. He'd lift his nose and stick his neck and head out and bawl; his flanks and diaphragm would heave like a bellows when he did.

It was a sunny fall day, but chilly. I'd been wet and cold and it took the heat of the fire a while to reach right to the small of my back so that I could feel it. "We'll have to come back tomorrow or the next day and gather them all over again," I thought. "Shouldn't be too bad, though, if they don't cross back over the river."

I looked at the river, and at the body, and off at the desert on the other side of the river, and at the mountains beyond that: Bly Mountain, and two or three smaller ones. It was a broken-up, tilted desert, where there'd been a few volcanoes in the old days, and wherever you looked you could see a lot of it—not like a flatland desert where the horizon cuts it off and takes it away from you. I couldn't say if I felt good, bad, glad, or sorry, but I know I did feel sort of taken out of everyday.

Our horses stood hobbled a little ways off and far enough apart so that they wouldn't pester each other, except for Larry's horse; we'd left him loose, and he was standing rubbed up against Roy's horse, who he'd been raised with. He was wet and shivering, and kept shaking his head and neck even yet, trying to get the water out of his ears.

"We'd better start *him* drying out, too, while we're waiting," Roy said, and nodded in the direction of Larry.

"When I hired onto this place they told me I'd have to do a little of everything," Gordon said.

"It's noon, Gordon," I said, "so you can carry him on your own time."

"Don't know if that's better or worse," he said.

"Well when you figure it out keep it to yourself," I said.

We used to go round and round, Gordon and I, mostly just to make the time pass, driving cattle.

We broke the branches off a chokecherry bush and made a bed for him by the fire—to raise him up so he'd dry faster and cleaner. Talked about undressing him and drying the clothes separately, but that turned out to be all talk: after we carried him up there, bleating like a bunch of sheep because of our feet, and laid him on the branches, no one said any more about taking his clothes off.

All this time Ben hadn't said a word, and we all noticed he didn't look as if he felt right. None of us knew the man; I'd talked to him two or three different times, which was more than anyone else had. Anyhow, he looked now like a man who wanted to be let alone; and so we did, at least at first.

He was the kind who'd talk to you, friendly-like, but if you looked at his face when he was just riding along thinking his own thoughts, he looked like a worrier. And it turned out he was—one of those self-punishers. He'd brood and brood and generally had something to brood about, and made it worse for himself in the process. He'd get a woman, for example, then drive her off by staying home and being so damn gloomy all the time, never taking her anywhere and hardly able to listen to what she'd say when she talked.

And he fulminated so hard inside his own mind—blaming his ulcer, his poverty, his bad thoughts, and everything else on himself one minute, then blaming fate for being so hard on him in particular the next—that he finally could hardly get anything at all passed through his stomach. Ruined it. Drank too, at one time, they say, but he quit that for good before I ever met him. But I don't say he was any worse than the rest of us.

We all backed up to the fire again, with Ben standing farthest from it, though he looked as if he needed the warmth worse than we did.

"Looks almost intelligent," Gordon said.

I turned and looked at the corpse. "He does," I said. "I noticed that."

"Having his mouth and his eyes closed helps," Gordon said.

I didn't say anything, but I couldn't help thinking Gordon was right about that, too.

Alive he'd gone around with his mouth half open looking puzzled—hard to say what by; everything, I guess, because he never paid enough attention to any particular thing to be puzzled by it. If you asked him to do the simplest thing—something a dog could do, like to plant himself in an open gate so the cattle would walk past the gate instead of through it, he'd nod and grin and then go stand in the middle of the road and turn all the cattle through the gate. Yet you knew he shouldn't have been that dumb; and half the time when I looked at his face I wanted to slap it and see if I couldn't just wake him up.

But I never did, and now he looked the way I'd always thought he should have looked—though I never could have pictured it. That muscle that pulled his mouth into that puzzled expression was out of commission; still, you'd think all those years of looking stupid would have made a permanent mark. His hair was plastered wet to his head, which gave him a longer forehead than I remembered, and his nose looked sharper and longer, as I suppose a dead person's will generally—they lie so flat and straight, facing straight up, with the head so still, and the face a little gaunt. But while I was standing there watching him, I began to think his color improved, either like ours did, from the warmth—or maybe the flames reflecting off his skin just made it look so. But Ben, when I looked at him, still looked as pale as we all had just after we'd come out of the water.

"Anybody besides you take offense if I eat?" Gordon said.

"They'll take offense whether you eat or not," I said.

Roy said we might as well eat all right, since it was time, and while we were waiting to dry out—our clothes he meant—and after that two of us could start for town.

Ben glanced up whenever anyone said anything, and that was all.

"You look a little pale around the gills, Ben," I said finally. "You not feeling well?"

"Not so hot," he said. "I'll be okay."

"Enough to make a man's stomach do flip-flops, something like that happening," I said.

"You bet it is," Roy said.

Ben smiled a little, or attempted to smile, like a person trying to be friendly, or anyway not to be unfriendly.

The lunches were tied to our saddles; our socks were still wet, and Ben had pulled his boots back off, so it meant another barefooted walk for somebody. "Draw you straws," I said.

I broke up a twig. Broke it into four, but I couldn't make up my mind whether to put Ben in the draw or leave him out; sometimes a person hates to be left out, even of things he doesn't want to be in on.

"I'll pass, Murphy," he said.

"Don't blame you," I said.

"Heck no," Roy said.

Roy lost the draw. Best that way, since he was the lightest on his feet. I watched him pick his way, sort of helping him along mentally. Larry's horse was still huddled up against Roy's horse; he was drawn at the flanks and it seemed as if the longer he stood there the more he hunched up—so that now the back of the saddle pointed up off his back like a piece of cardboard. Roy noticed it too, and while he was over there he uncinched Larry's saddle and carried it back over to the fire, holding it in one hand and braced against his hip, while he had the four sack lunches from the other saddles piled up along his other arm. He'd doubled the cinch up so it wouldn't drag, but it still snagged a couple of bushes along the way and he had to stop and tease it loose.

I watched it all—we all did. I saw Roy uncinch the saddle, and I saw the looks on their faces watching him—plain attention on Gordon's, and something more than that on Ben's, unless hindsight makes me think so. But right at that time I didn't think even to wonder about the cinch myself—whether it was loose or tight—and Roy told me later he didn't notice himself which it was.

Roy rolled Larry's saddle over on its side by the fire; there, still tied to the saddle swell, was his sack lunch, all soaked through and bloated.

"Hell of a time to die, right before lunch," Gordon said, "especially for him."

"Liked his lunch all right, sure did," Roy said.

"Last thing I heard him say, come to think of it," I said, "'How close is it to noon?'"

"He'd generally say that three or four times between ten and twelve," Roy said.

"He'd mash it though, before he ever got a chance to eat it," Gordon said.

"Wasn't because he didn't like it," I said. "Just the opposite: didn't want to lose it."

"I know that," Gordon said. "I wonder what the hell ever made him like he was."

"Ask him," I said, just to be smart. But then I looked over at his face myself, as if I thought I might learn something, though I didn't even know what I wanted to learn.

Ben was sitting back a little ways, still pale and hanging his head; if I'd had any sense, the way his eyes flicked up every time somebody said something would have scared me. It did bother me a little, that he couldn't seem to make himself be either in or out of things.

"Ben, you weren't around Larry much," I said, "but we used to say to him, 'Larry, when are you going to stop asking when's lunch?' 'After lunch!' he'd say, and laugh. Remember that, Roy?"

Ben looked up at me. "I didn't think he had that much wit," he said, and I was kind of glad to hear him say anything.

"Roy here taught him the answer," I said. "Should we take his lunch off the saddle and throw it in the fire? Might make his mother feel worse, to see it come back with him. She may as well think he ate it."

"I'll do that," Ben said. You could see he was trying hard to pull himself together. But when he crouched down by the saddle and tried to untie those wet leather saddle strings, his hands shook so much I was embarrassed for the man.

"Look at the way he cinched his lunch down," I said. "Same as always. Here." I cut the lunch in two with my pocket knife; it pulled apart like a hunk of mud, which it just about was, and I threw the two pieces in the fire. "His mother packs him a good one," I said.

"Doesn't look too good to me," Gordon said.

"Well, you're so goddamned particular," I said.

"I remember one morning," Roy said, "we were saddling our horses and I said to him, 'Larry, how would you like me to show you a way to tie your lunch to your saddle so you won't squash it.' 'Thanks, Roy, sure,' he said."

"Step on his toe and he'd thank you for it," Gordon said.

"I showed him, and he did it himself afterwards," Roy said, "But the lesson never took. Went right back to his own method."

We talked, not thinking we were saying anything much. Ben was sitting to my left, Gordon to my right, and the body off just beyond him, so that whenever I turned to talk or argue with Gordon I could see it. The eyes were shut, but not quite all the way—looked like the man on the post office porch who they always show in the movies, the one who pretends to be taking a nap while he's really peeking at you out from under his eyelids, watching everything.

"He had a passion for cinching things down," Gordon said, "couldn't help himself," and he nodded toward Larry's saddle. Gordon was just speculating and trying to appear wise; he'd been way across the river himself, where he couldn't see anything.

"I was watching him," Ben said, in a thin voice that sounded as if it came up out of a hole.

We all turned and looked at him. But Gordon answered him just as though he thought they were having an everyday conversation. "I was watching him too," he said. "I know he got off and fooled with it."

Ben lowered his chin and drew a line in the dirt with his finger. He had one leg stretched out flat on the ground and the other one drawn up to his chest so that his chin was almost on his knee (he was so long and limber-jointed that sometimes when you looked at him you'd think bones and joints and maybe a few wires to work them with was all that was there). His jaws were clamped so tight that the ridge where his teeth met ran all the way to his ears, and he was pale; he looked bad, but since he hadn't looked too good earlier either, I didn't make much of it. I went on talking to Gordon.

"Well, why would he get off and fool with it?" I said, "if he wasn't making it looser?" I looked past him at Larry. "What else would the poor boy be doing, Gordon?"

"Pulling it tight," Gordon said.

I saw Roy tilt his head. I looked at Ben. His chin had sunk so low you couldn't see his face for his hat; he had one hand wrapped around his ankle like a monkey, and the other one was still in the dirt but wasn't moving. "Sick for a fact," I thought. "But there's nothing I can do about it," I said to myself, and turned away.

"Pulling it tight without thinking, you mean?" I said to Gordon, and when I looked back at Larry I couldn't help thinking he'd changed his expression.

"Without or with, either way—wasn't much of a thinker," Gordon said. I started to believe I saw Larry frown then, right while I was looking at him—and if he'd opened one eye, I wouldn't have been surprised.

It was my mind doing it, I knew that. Like when a flame or the shadow of a flame seems to flicker in time to a song playing on the radio: you know it's your mind that can't leave two things alone to happen at the same time without trying to make them have to do with each other. But I still kept hoping if I looked close enough I'd get a hint. Had he tightened the cinch, or loosened it? Had the old horse maybe swum into a snag everyone else and all the cattle had missed? Or had the horse not started to swim yet and stepped too hard on a rock that slipped out from under him? Not that it made a whole hell of a lot of difference, but I wanted to know. And I forgot to look at Ben at all.

"Still seems unlikely he'd get off intending to loosen it, and then tighten it," I said to Gordon.

"Seems unlikely the horse would roll over in the water and drown him, but he did," Gordon said.

"That's true too," I said, and looked at Larry hard; but he was mum.

So I looked across at Roy. "You happen to notice, Roy?" I said. "You pulled the saddle off."

Roy gave his head a little shake like a man with a fly on his nose—meaning I should shut my mouth. I swung my head in Ben's direction just as he jumped up on his feet; he stood stock still with his arms stiff by his sides, opening and closing both hands like a machine: looked like a man plugged into a light socket, the way they show it in the funny papers. I never saw so much tension with so little motion—though there was plenty of motion in those hands. "I was watching him," he said, this time in a voice so choked off you could hardly understand him.

Roy and I just opened our mouths and sat there, but Gordon got up and started waving his arm. "Oh wait now," he said. "I never meant to think you weren't keeping an eye on him. If you saw him loosen his cinch he loosened it."

"Horse may have lost his footing," I said.

"Sure may have," Gordon said.

"You happen to remember, Roy, if it was loose?" I said.

"Sure was, now that I think about it," he said, nodding as if he thought Ben was deaf.

Poor Ben opened his mouth to speak and couldn't say a word. He looked down at his hands, which were still going, if a little slower, and which Gordon and Roy and I couldn't take our eyes off in spite of ourselves. He looked down at them, and you could almost see him willing them to stop. One stopped; the other went on a few strokes by itself, as if it had hold of a cow's teat.

"Misunderstanding," he said, and shook his head trying to clear it.

"All a misunderstanding, friend," Gordon said; "think nothing of it and I won't either." And he tiptoed over and held his big hand out, which Ben shook.

A couple of weeks after the drowning Gordon and I were out trying to restring an old stretch of wire fence.

"Okay, now see if you can just pull the sag out of it," I said.

He took hold of the strand of wire with the pliers, pulled it, and then pulled it a little more, so the old rust-brittle thing broke and fell in two pieces on the ground.

"Trouble with you is you don't know loose from tight," I said.

"I still think he pulled it tight," he said, "—just between us."

I didn't say anything, but as time went by I leaned that way myself.

The Sinner

Later on, Ben's girlfriend Toni would confide in me. I was good for that: I believed fanatically in keeping secrets, and loved the attention—especially when it came from her.

But at first, before Toni took the trouble to win me over, I was naturally jealous. This took the form of disapproval. Having reached the age of ten I was fully civilized and had *morals*. I disapproved of the way Ben carried on with women, and in fact I learned the terms of my disapproval from him, though the feelings were my own. He was always full of remorse after he went out.

When he went out he drank, and when he drank he was unpleasant, and from all reports they (the women, at the time chiefly Toni) saved him from his worst excesses: coaxed him and his imagined enemies away from fights, tricked or begged his money away from him (he often had seven or eight hundred dollars with him when he went out dancing on weekends, and when he was drunk he'd insist—very belligerently—on treating everyone he saw, if he didn't want to fight them instead). But the women were *there* when he fell and to my mind were responsible for the trouble they prevented and more besides.

Ben himself, when they weren't around, spoke ironically of "cigarettes and whiskey and wild wild women," and "girlin'," and whenever the popular western song "I'm Drivin' the Nails in My Coffin" (which had to do with drink and women) came on the radio, Ben would switch it off.

It was a puzzle to me. Since Ben was a hero in my eyes and by no means a weak-willed man (nor was he weak-willed in reality), I didn't understand why he didn't just put a stop to the nonsense.

Ben had been married twice, and seven years after this, when he was over fifty, would marry again. But for fifteen years he was a bachelor, and at the time I'm talking about certainly led the life of one. He hardly allowed anyone—men or women—into his house, in which he didn't so much live as just slept, and *that* not regularly. I'd hung around his riding stables close to a year and had never been inside the place—nor ever was to be, though I was in many other houses of his later.

One Friday afternoon Ben asked me to wake him when I came over to the stables the next morning. Usually he'd be up long before I got there, unless he was hung over, and so I knew he must be planning to go out.

Even when the time came, it seemed like an easy enough thing to do, and only when I'd walked down the path to the house and stood looking at the door I was supposed to knock on did I begin to have qualms. The house was an old frame one, set on the dry hillside; nothing grew around it; the shades were drawn on the three or four visible windows, and there was no noise—just the heavy buzz of a summer morning. A cat dropped from the roof, scaring me; it rubbed up around my legs, whining, and evidently wanted to be fed.

I'd brought myself nearly to the point, I think, of knocking, when I did distinguish from the insects another sound; and as it is with sounds, once I was sure I'd heard it I couldn't stop hearing it. For a moment or two I rather stupidly couldn't make out what it was: something between purring and groaning and varying from instant to instant in loudness and evenness. We had an old dog at home that made a similar racket when it lay on its side and slept; but only when I realized that the sound came from one of the windows, which must have been open behind the shade, did I understand that this was Ben sleeping. The irreverent phrase "the old man is snoring" came into my head.

Was I really to knock and wake him? I knew such things were done, but by older, bolder people—not by me. I tried to remember the exact instruction, to see if there wasn't some way out of it: "Maxie, I want you to do something for me if you're here in the morning." "I will be." "I kind of thought so. Well, you come on down to the house and get me up, will you?—just as early as you get over here." Casual, but plain. I tapped, mouselike, on the door. Nothing.

I tapped again, more loudly, waited, and then knocked more loudly still. But beyond a certain intensity—about the loudness and rhythm of normal discreet knocking—I couldn't make myself go. There was no result.

The hungry cat rubbed against me; I tried to kick it, but it was too close and I could only shove it with my foot, which had as little effect as my knocking and helped bring me to a pitch of helpless exasperation. In a kind of daze, afraid to rap louder and afraid to abandon the job, I began to tap along steadily like a woodpecker. At last it seemed to me that I'd heard something and I stopped. What I'd heard was a cessation of sound. I could hear no breathing now, no groaning, nothing. But no—now there it was—it had begun again— he was still asleep. I held my breath and rapped. The bedsprings creaked. I stopped. Silence. I knocked. Then there was a terrifying racket that made me jerk and jump backward. A snorting and snarl- ing and creaking of springs—as if I'd stuck a pitchfork into a bear. It subsided, and fortunately—as I felt at the moment—a more or less ordinary snoring took its place.

I stood there suffering for what seemed a long time. I screwed up my courage by remembering my instructions and by imagining all sorts of reprimands I'd get for not doing what I was asked. "Okay," I said to myself, "just once more." I knocked, more softly than I in- tended, but he was attuned to it now. This time within the half- groan half-snarl that he let out I recognized a bit of smothered human speech: "Damn it! Who's there?" I don't think any process of thought could have induced me to knock again, but I stood there a minute or two, afraid to walk away, and when I did I wandered off indecisively, pulling at weeds and kicking clods.

I hung around the barn. I couldn't bring myself to do anything. I thought of going home and pretending I'd never come; or of going back up to the house, rapping boldly on his window—"Ben, hey Ben! Come on, it's nine o'clock. You wanted me to wake you." And I thought of working: if he saw me working he might tend to forgive me; besides, there was much to be done. But wander around and think, and sit and think, was all I did, and my thoughts were useless. An hour and a half later, he got up.

His hat pulled down and head bent—so that his face looked like a long nose hovering over a long chin with a barely visible straight line marking the lips—he came walking slowly down the hill to the barn. At the same time a car pulled into the lot and a couple of customers got out. The horses hadn't even been fed yet, let alone caught and saddled—and it was a Saturday!

I appeared from around a corner of the barn. "Morning," he said, lips hardly moving, and nodded. Much as I feared a reprimand, it was impossible to mistake this sour greeting for one (in any case, I probably more feared than really expected one). I understood that his mind was turning on matters of its own and had no space for my transgressions.

"Morning, what can I do for you?" he said to the customers, two college-age girls. Ben glanced at their clothes—new jeans and old baggy mens' shirts—and at the way they stood—at once posed and awkward—in their western boots, and as he always did he mentally selected horses for them.

"We'd like two horses for an hour, please," said one.

"All right, we'll sure fix you up with a couple."

"We're experienced riders," said the same girl. Someone had probably told her that this is what you have to say in order to get a "good" horse.

"Are you? That's all right," Ben said, without irony but absently. "Go catch Sonny and Shorty for me, will you, son?" This was a dog-gentle pair, immune to everything and always given to beginners.

"Are those good horses?" said the Experienced Rider suspiciously. "Sure are," Ben said, truly enough. "We're a little late getting around this morning. You ladies just sit down a minute if you want to and we'll get you set up."

He turned and headed for the barn—I wondered why—and at the

same time that I went after the horses he disappeared around the side of it. When I came back leading Sonny and Shorty I saw that both of the Dutch doors of a stall were pulled shut. The bottom door opened and, ducking down and pulling down his hat, he came out, white in the face and wiping his mouth with a handkerchief. He looked at me, shook his head, as if at the fool he was, and stuffed his handkerchief back in his pocket.

"How're those stirrups?" he said to the same girl after she'd struggled heavily up onto the small horse. "A little short, are they?"

"No, I think they're all right, thank you," she said.

"Why don't you stand up in them once, just to make sure?"

She stood up, so high that she lost her balance and had to reach out suddenly and catch herself on Sonny's neck.

"Maybe we ought to put them down a notch or two, what do you think?" Ben said.

She had blanched with the loss of balance; now she pinkened and shrugged. While she sat there passively, he lifted her foot out of the stirrup, which he then let down several notches, guided her foot back into it, and went around to the other side to do the same.

"Now that's about got her, has it?" he said.

She stood up again, with relative grace. "I think so, yes," she said, once more self-possessed.

Ben put in his day, saying no more than he felt he had to to anyone, and every hour or two he turned aside and took a soda pill.

In the middle of the afternoon Toni and her friend Shirley came along, and everything changed. All day cars had been pulling into the lot down below the barn. We could see the lot from the hitchrack, and I looked at each car with some curiosity to see what sort of customers would get out of it. Ben usually did too, but today as far as I could tell he didn't, and hardly took an interest in anything beyond his stomach and his thoughts.

He was just starting negotiations with a whole family of riders, and I stood by to see what horses he'd use. I guess he must have heard the faint whirr of the motor coming up the hill and recognized it; he stopped talking and lifted his head like a bird dog. I looked in that direction (even the father of the family did), and there was Toni's car, which I'd seen a couple of times before, cresting the hill. Ben excused himself, said he'd be right back, and just walked off.

I was determined to carry on but soon came to a sticking point—which saddle to put on Dan (I really wanted to go after Ben anyway)—and followed to ask. He went off frivolously, I in the line of duty.

"Well, for a couple of drunks you girls seem to be tracking pretty straight today," I heard him say. And I'd hoped to the last that he had—or at least for shame's sake would invent—something important to say.

Toni and her shadow Shirley laughed. I watched as Toni clicked her heels together, bowed impressively, extended her hand palm upward, and said in a deep, drawling, mimicking voice—apparently in imitation of the bandleader of the night before—"Howdy folks! And I'd *liiike* you to *meet* . . . the *boys* in the *band*."

And at this Ben—instead of turning away in disgust—grinned, for the first time all day.

Toni, who'd seen me two or three times before, attempted to look at me in a friendly fashion. I looked away, refused to meet her eyes, and showed her the face of stone she deserved.

If this set her back she didn't show it. They laughed again, at nothing so far as I could see—and I certainly hadn't missed anything.

Toni glanced up at Ben's hat; she whispered something in Shirley's ear. Shirley looked, clapped her hand over her mouth, and said, "He did! He lost it!" and went off into gales of laughter.

Ben looked puzzled. "Who lost what?" he said rather gruffly.

Shirley bent over, convulsed with laughter which, as I could see, she only pretended to try to repress, covering her mouth with her hand.

A look of comprehension passed over Ben's face; he touched the band of his hat. "This isn't my town hat," he said. (I eventually figured out that some meaningful trinket had been stuck in his hatband the night before, and it was this they thought he'd lost.) "You think I'd wear an old sow-slopper like this to the big Friday night?

That's the sweat of the brow—" he pointed to a place low on the crown where little peaks of dark stain rose up. "There's a time and place for everything."

At this, more laughter.

"Ben—" I said.

"Just like my mother used to tell my father," he went on, "when they were getting ready to go to town. 'Well, let's go!' he'd say, just come in out of the field and dirty all over.

"'Go where? You wash your head before you go to town with me!'"

"Did he?" Toni said.

"'Nobody there cares what I wash,'" he'd say, 'they just want to see some of that *long green.*'

"'They won't see much when *you* get there,' my mother'd say."

"Did he wash his head?" Toni said.

"Not unless he felt like it."

"I'll bet he felt like it though," Toni said.

"Ben—" I said.

"It looks just like the other hat to me," Toni said.

"Me too," Shirley said. (In fact all his hats—dress and work—were exactly alike except as to cleanness and newness.)

"That just goes to show," Ben said, "you don't neither one of you know S from S."

This bit of pointless coyness annoyed me more than anything.

"Ben—"

"What is it, son?" he said, irritated.

"Which saddle do you want on Dan?"

"Why just the same one we always put on him."

"But remember, he has that sore."

"Uh-huh; I'll be along in a minute," he said indifferently.

Untrue to his gloom, his work, and me. He was a lost soul. When he came back, not long after I did, I couldn't bring myself to speak or even to look at him. (Since I hardly ever spoke anyway, this spleen of mine, which lasted an hour or more, may not have been noticed.)

Toni and Shirley could ride. Ben insisted that they use his own saddles—not the rent-string ones but his very own private ones—

even though they had their own in the car. They rode the same horses as usual—Apple and Stony—who were so lively that there were rarely customers capable enough.

Off by themselves, out of the way, by the trail that started down into the canyon, they tethered these horses to a sumac bush and saddled them, while Ben and I worked. I could see them brushing the horses off, jabbering to each other, fooling with the saddles, bridles, and blankets, and laughing—at nothing no doubt. I disapproved of Ben for continually looking over at them. (I was aware that I did the same, but since I had unfriendly feelings it was all right.)

I admired Toni unhappily as she got on Stony. She slipped her slender foot into the stirrup, gathered up the reins on the fidgety horse and checked him at the same time that she easily swung her long leg over the cantle, and then unconsciously and without a false move found the off stirrup with her boot—better than it's done in the movies, where I'd already noticed that everyone but the extras fumbled. Female silliness and such abilities ought *not* to coincide.

I'd caught Dan and now I saddled him. To comfort myself I imagined how one day *it would all be found out.* Just what, I couldn't have said, but it all would. Ben would find it out—what they were really worth—and apologize to me (I couldn't have said for what), and although he wouldn't be able to quite forgive himself for his philanderings, I would forgive him.

My injured mood wore away, though I hung onto it as best I could. Five-thirty came; the stream of customers had dwindled, and Ben closed the stables: he turned over the sign that hung on the outside wall of the office and said OPEN on one side and CLOSED MONDAYS on the other. People were supposed to divine that "Closed Mondays" meant "Closed"—and I remember how stupid I used to think they were when they appeared to be in doubt. But we had a new sign that as a concession to the public Ben had had Shirley paint—STABLES CLOSED—and that Ben had mounted on a rubber tire. I rolled this down to the parking lot. Half an hour later the chores were all done and we were at our leisure.

This was my favorite time of day. The work was done but the day wasn't over—the work itself wasn't really *over,* as my tired legs and face caked with dust testified. Ben would take his ease, his pockets stuffed with money—*cash money* as he called it—and after a busy day like today some of this money was not just cash but "to the good."

It was also the time of day when friends of Ben's were most likely to visit. I had my own way of picturing this: we sat around together—Ben and I—and whoever came by was visiting *us*. In general these visitors, who after they'd seen me a few times could read me like a book, would humor me, and Ben himself used to kiddingly call me "the foreman," because of this visible self-importance of mine. And it's true, at this time of day I often felt that I was really somebody. In the morning, on the other hand, I'd often arrive reduced—simply by the night's separation—to a moral rag, so that I showed up half expecting to be sent home again and occasionally even had flashes of dreamlike fear that he wouldn't recognize me. (The following winter something no better actually happened: after missing a few days I went over to the stables and found Ben and his belongings gone, moved out—no one could tell me where.)

Ben sat in a chair in front of the office, looking over the day's accounts, one skinny leg hung limberly over the thigh of the other, and swinging his foot. In order to get as much distance between himself and the written word as possible, he tilted the daybook backward on his knee and tilted his head back, and also, for some reason—maybe because he was more farsighted on one side than the other—cocked his head at an angle. He looked as if he were sighting down his nose trying to draw a bead on this dance of names and numbers. He moved a forefinger slowly down the rightmost column—the cash column—which must have been long.

I sat on the bench in front of the office, playing with a little old lariat Ben had given me, trying to rope a pail; since I was too lazy to stand up and couldn't swing the rope sitting down without hitting the wall behind me, I was having even less luck than usual—though I cared less as well.

Toni and Shirley were still out riding.

A truck came rattling up into the lot. We both looked up and Ben lost his place. "Here's Spaeth," he said, and went back to his ledger.

Jerry came up the path, walking in his awkwardly springy way on the balls of his feet, wearing street shoes and a ball cap, a cigar in his mouth. When he got close I could see his gold teeth, which I never tired of looking at. He was Ben's friend and traded horses for a living.

"Hi, Spaeth," Ben said.

"How're you boys getting along today?" Jerry said.

"Fine," I said, throwing the rope at the pail and missing.

"You get any work out of this old man?" he said.

"Pretty much," I said shyly. By this time I'd decided he was admirable in spite of his uncowboylike clothes (he was a horse trader, after all) and so I was a little intimidated by him, though he was one of the least awesome of men and one of the kindest—as I also felt.

"Look in the icebox in there and see if you can find yourself a beer," Ben said. "I'll be through with this in a minute."

"Counting your money, are you?"

"Lots of numbers and not many dollars," Ben said, stopping his finger. "That's how it is renting out these pissheads. Anyway, middle man gets it all."

"That right?" Jerry said, "and here I thought I was one." He turned to me again: "You'd think the old feller wasn't stuffing his sock," he said, nodding toward Ben and winking. "You got any ice in that icebox or just beer?"

"I think there's some," I said.

Jerry got up to break himself off a piece of ice, which he would then stuff into one side of his mouth—though Ben said it was made from dirty water.

"You keep out of that ice," Ben said.

"Just count your money, I won't eat much," said Jerry, and went into the office.

I looked up. This time I'd seen them as soon as Ben, if not before. They were coming up the trail.

The sweaty necks of the horses were stretched out low with the effort of climbing, and their legs, which must have begun to sweat only with the last efforts of the climb, were so freshly damp—no dust having had time to stick to them yet—that they glistened; the cords above the working knees shifted under the skin and made it ripple. Toni and Shirley half stood in the stirrups and leaned a little ahead to make their weight as easy to bear as possible; their backs, though angled forward, were straight as stalks.

I reminded myself I had something against them, but it bothered me that in my improved mood I could no longer remember just what it was.

Jerry came out with the ice in his mouth. "Now he'll lay that book down, won't he," he said, ostensibly to me; then directly to Ben: "I was worried you might have to buy you another horse or two to get rid of all that money you're making, but now I see."

They rode into the barnyard and Jerry took off his cap and said hello—he'd met them both before. A little small talk was made about the ride; they unsaddled and led the horses around a bit until they were cool and the sweat had dried. Ben sat in his chair and watched them and talked to Jerry, who watched both the women and the horses.

Toni and Shirley ran some water on the salty, curdled-looking backs and tied the horses to the hitchrack. They sat down on the wooden platform that extended out from the tack room. Jerry Spaeth, who was about Ben's age and married—the girls were twenty years younger—took a couple of cigars from his pocket and extended one around, gesturing slowly toward each of us in turn.

I shook my head.

Shirley shook her head and giggled.

"Don't tempt me," Toni said, "I'm a lady."

"I'll vouch for it," Ben said, with some self-directed irony, as Toni, whose husband was away in the army, had unshakeable convictions as to what constituted married loyalty and the self-possession to abide by them. "I think I'll have a cigarette, Jerry," Ben said, and to Shirley and Toni: "Want one?"

Shirley shook her head.

"Sure," said Toni. "Mine are in the car."

"Ah, let those tailormades lie. Here—I'll build you one." Ben pulled a tiny yellow string that stuck out of his shirt pocket and fished out a bag of tobacco and from under it a slim sheaf of papers.

"I want to do it," Toni said; "you said you'd teach me how."

"Did I say that? All right, well now's the time. —If you folks don't mind?" he added with pointless gallantry. He came over and sat down next to her on the edge of the platform and gave her a couple of papers which he showed her how to seam together. "Just do as I say and as I do," he said.

"I'll try," she said, and moved closer to him. I watched their knees touch; as if this broke some small barrier, she laid her head against his shoulder and rubbed upward like a cat until the top of her head touched the under brim of his hat.

He loosened the drawstring on the tobacco sack. I was fascinated by these little bags and used to pick up his empty ones—though I could never think of any use for them, and lost interest when they were mine and safe in my room at home. The tiny yellow drawstring was twisted in strands like a real rope, the bag itself made of white cotton like that of a flour sack but thinner and even softer; but best of all, stamped on the cloth was the tiny figure of a red bull.

Ben gently tapped a little tobacco out into the cupped paper, passed the bag to her, and watched as she did the same. "Atta girl—we'll turn you into a cowgirl yet," he said.

He slowly rolled the filled paper back and forth in his fingers, and after packing it in this way finally rolled it into a tube that only needed to be sealed. She imitated him, and when he lifted the cigarette to his mouth and ran the remaining edge of paper along the tip of his tongue, she did the same, rolling her eyes to the side to watch.

Both Ben and Jerry complimented her. Ben lit it for her, and lit his own. After a puff or two Toni started running her tongue in and out of her mouth, twisting it between her teeth and finally spitting.

"You don't much like that old Bull Durham tobacco raw, do you?" Jerry said. "I don't blame you. Better rinse your mouth out with one of these." He waved his cigar.

Toni threw the cigarette down and ground it under the sole of her boot, laughing and making a face. "Guess I'll never make a cowgirl," she said. "Sorry!"

"Or be one either," Ben said wryly. "You didn't do so bad. Here, you want me to roll one for you now?"

"Phaa!" she said. She stuck her tongue out and picked off a grain of tobacco, which she wiped onto her pants. "I'll stick to my what-do-you-call-thems."

"Storeboughts," Jerry said.

"Tailormades," Ben said.

"Them are best," Jerry said. "Old Ben here, he thinks he's still back in Colorada."

She walked down to her car for her cigarettes. When she came back she stopped and passed her hand over Stony's drying back.

"Well, what do you think—" Ben said to them, "you girls ready to make another sashay downtown and around tonight?"

"I hope to tell you," Toni said.

"Me too," Shirley said, and giggled.

"Better come along downtown with us, Spaeth," Ben said, just to be polite.

"That would be nice," Toni said, with considerably more enthusiasm.

Jerry looked up at her. "I know someone who might not think so," he said.

"Oh—well go get her!" said Toni.

"No—but I'm much obliged," Jerry said—this with a curious change of tone or excess of feeling, as if surprised to find that this attractive woman really had friendly feelings toward him. "And I don't mean to you, you old bastard," he said to Ben, obviously intending to be good-natured; but it didn't come out quite right, and Ben looked at him surprised.

The horses were dry. They brushed them down and led them off toward the big rent-horse corral to turn them loose.

It struck me that we'd already fed the other horses and they'd all been eating for a good thirty minutes. "Will Stony and Apple get enough hay?" I asked Ben.

"That's about all those two do anyway is eat," he said—this was just rhetoric uttered while he thought it over. "I'll tell you what, son, would you mind running up there; tell those girls I said to put the horses in a couple of empty stalls so they won't get shorted. I'll get up and go throw them a flake of hay in a bit."

"Okay. Is it okay if *I* feed them?"

"If you want to, you bet it is. Maybe if you look at those girls just right you'll get a little help."

"Just sort of close one eye," Jerry said.

I wanted to deny that I would look at anyone "right," least of all them, in order to get something done for me, but I recognized if not that this was foolish at least that it would sound awfully foolish to say, and so, irritated, I ran off to catch them before they unbridled the horses.

Toni was just opening the gate. "Ben said to put them in stalls so they can eat," I said abruptly. "I'll go get them some hay." But I stood there and watched her to make sure she latched the gate properly.

"Okay, that's a good idea," Toni said. She looked at me, I looked down. I wanted to say it was really my idea, and had to remind myself just how little I cared for her opinion of me.

"There's a couple of empty stalls on this end," I said.

They went toward the barn with the horses; I went to the haypile. I'd just rolled a new bale down from the stack and was twisting a hayhook in one of the wires to break it when Toni, who I hadn't seen come up, said, "Can I help you?"

"I can get it," I said in a monotone that I tried to drive all feeling from and make like ice—but it came out peevish.

"So can I," she said.

I gave the hook a savage twist and popped the wire. "I mean I don't mind doing it," I said, reddening.

"I don't either," she said. "How much do you think we should give them?"

"Haven't you ever fed horses?" I said, surprised.

"Oh sure, a lot of them. But you know, different hay is different, different horses are different; anyway, some places they feed them a lot in the morning and less at night—usually mostly at night, most places, but I mean you never know—"

"This Imperial Valley hay is really strong," I said, repeating what I'd heard. "It's almost all leaves."

She reached down and skimmed the top of the broken bale with her fingers until she found a place where the tightly packed hay could easily be parted, spread it, and pulled some out and put it in her mouth.

"Do you like to ride?" she said.

"I like to ride after cattle," I said (neglecting to mention that so far I never had).

"Well, if Ben gets his ranch maybe he'll hire you."

"A *ranch?* Do you think he'll get one?" I said excitedly. I'd never heard of this ambition of Ben's.

"I don't know. If he doesn't give all his money away he probably will. He'd like to."

"I know," I said.

She separated off a thick wedge of hay from the end of the bale. "Here—do you think this is too much for one of them?"

I looked, more intent on the wise and speculative way I cocked my head and said "That looks about right" than on the estimation itself.

She bent down to gather it up. I separated some in the same way, for the other horse, and picked it up, apprehensive now as to whether it would be the same size as her portion. We faced each other over our armloads of hay. I turned my eyes down—she was looking at me again—and looked at her hay, then mine. I had picked up too much; in fact I could hardly keep my arms around it and was being prickled unpleasantly. I waited for her to turn and walk off. She didn't, and it seemed to me that she was as if by magic demanding that I look at her. I backed up a step—there was only about a foot between us (or at least between our hay)—but I couldn't turn, it was impossible to turn around and walk off, and yet I knew better than to look at her.

My eyes were drawn upward. She was looking at me steadily. I looked at her eyes and then tried to shift to her mouth, which still had a couple of green twigs sticking out of it—she'd eaten the leaves. Her lips smiled and moved and were impossible to look at, and the eyes, which I'd never got entirely clear of, drew me back. Her eyes were luminous and serious; in reality she just looked friendlily into mine and not for any very long time. "I forget which stall they're in," she said; "you go first."

She melted me like butter.

When we went back to the tack room where Jerry and Ben were still sitting, I didn't trail or lead her but walked right beside.

"Get your chores done?" Ben said.

"Oop—I left the bridle somewhere," Toni said.

"Want me to get it for you?" I said.

"No, but you can come help me," she said.

"Help you what?" Ben said. "We're going to have to keep an eye on you two now, I can see that."

"He must have did what I told him," Jerry said. "Don't know why it never worked for me—except for just that one time."

"Took all right, that once, didn't it?" Ben said.

"Come on," Toni said, "let the old folks talk."

"Okay," I said. Already having blushed, I proudly and self-consciously walked off with her.

From then on when she was at the stables I followed her around everywhere, dumbly and on the whole happily—like a sheep following a goat.

Eulogy

Fifteen years ago the boss's daughter Christine brought him home from college—big hardheaded boy named Johnny, about twenty-five or -six and already been in the service. Then she married him, and so Mr. Tedlock, since she was his only child and heir, didn't have much choice but to try to groom Johnny up to take over the ranch and run it.

So we had to start taking him with us when we went out to work. You couldn't teach him anything: he'd learn things, but all after his own fashion. He wasn't afraid of anything, and caused us no end of trouble. He'd catch a cow—usually a different one from the one he was aiming at—let her get away with his lariat around her neck, and we'd have to go get his rope back for him. Or we'd ask him to open a gate for the cattle to go through; he'd open it but only halfway, so that the cows naturally ripped it all apart going through—and we'd have to mend that. Or we'd have to bring back the cattle he'd driven four or five miles in the wrong direction and abandoned. We got too tired of him even to laugh at him. I used to hate to watch him get on a horse. Even someone who can't ride will figure out that climbing on a horse is just like climbing onto a ladder—you don't pull it over on yourself. But not him: instead of stepping up on one like anyone else, he'd take hold of the saddle horn and pull it toward him so hard the horse would groan and stumble sideways, unless the saddle turned first; but he learned to cinch that saddle so tight it's a wonder their hearts managed to beat. But he learned to ride quick enough— I mean, to stay on—and once he was on I used to hate to watch him

ride, too. Jarred the life out of their kidneys. The farm boss said he
was as hard on machines. Did everything by mainstrength, and he
had a lot of that.

Mr. Tedlock died, and we were working for Johnny. Wasn't a bad
manager: he'd learned the ranch, and ran it fine as a business. But
he didn't make a very nice boss.

For the first couple of years that he was running the place, we con-
soled ourselves he might get himself killed. The odds seemed against
it in one way: I've seen him with a half hitch around his belly bobbing like a cork, stretched out in the middle of a rope between an
eleven-hundred-pound horse and a thousand-pound cow, and both
of them jumping—and all it did for him was to keep him quiet for a
few minutes afterward. But on the other hand, he seemed bent on it
(and insofar as he was his own worst enemy we were all rooting for
him). He'd do little things that would get our hopes up: run a dirty
old nail through his foot and not go to a doctor. But our best hope in
those first couple of years after the old man died was for when Johnny'd get drunk and run his car off the road onto the desert in the
middle of the night. He piled up half a dozen cars and pickups. Gordon and Shorty and I had to go out and retrieve them, but we told
each other it was almost worth it.

Then one dark winter night he drove square into a juniper tree
and broke his back. For twenty-four hours the doctor wouldn't
vouch for his life. But in the end it paralyzed him from the waist
down and we were worse off than before.

Inside a month, after he'd learned how to scoot around the house
in his wheelchair, he began dealing on a pickup. When it came it was
all rigged up with a two-way radio and a telephone, four-wheel drive,
a winch, push-button brakes and gears—even had a siren, which
he'd turn on if you pretended you hadn't seen him. He couldn't go
everywhere a man could go on horseback, but close enough to it to
make you think so, so he was always occupying your mind. For a
while we hoped he might roll it over on himself or push the wrong
button and drive into the river. But that accident seemed to have
changed his attitude—wanted to live forever now.

He carried field glasses, and you couldn't sneak off for a nap or scratch yourself without he'd let you know about it later. I don't care if you were twenty miles out in the brush: you'd be thinking your own thoughts, look up, and that red pickup would be there on the nob of a hill that hadn't had anything on it a minute ago. The most ubiquitous man I ever heard of.

Went on like that for ten years, one very little different from the next. We'd put the cows out on the desert in the spring, in the fall bring them in to the meadows, where through the winter we'd feed them the hay the farm crew'd been putting up all summer. Johnny'd get a few boils from time to time, and that was the size of it.

Here last fall, one early morning, I threw my saddle and bedroll in the car and started down to the meadows. Way off across the desert was a big meadow ranch called the swamp, which belonged to Johnny and was about a hundred miles from the home ranch where he lived.

On my way out of town I stopped at the home ranch to take the mail down to the boys who were already at the meadows and any messages or bit of equipment that Johnny might want sent down if he wasn't going down early in the day himself. The garage door was closed—first thing I noticed when I pulled into the yard by Johnny's house. I looked at my watch: six-thirty. "Always out sticking his pickup's nose in things by this time," I said to myself.

I felt a little awkward about the notion of going up and knocking on the door so early in the morning. Usually Johnny'd have everything he wanted me to take right beside him on the seat of the truck. I looked for the hired man. Old pensioner who slept in a room on the end of one of the sheds. Wasn't a bad room, except Johnny'd drive his truck up within an inch of the outside wall and reach out and rap on the window glass above the man's bed. Anyhow, I couldn't find the hired man so I braved the house. I went to the kitchen door. There was a cardboard box with the mail in it on the steps, and then I saw the note tacked to the door.

"Murphy—" it began, and I looked and saw it was signed by

Duane, the hired man; so I tore it off and read it.

> Murphy—
>
> Christine asked me to tell you Johnny's in the hospital. He asked her
> to take him up sometime in the night. She said to tell you it's in his
> abdomen but they don't know yet what it is, took X-Rays or I don't
> what all and will take more tests or X-Rays this morning. So I hope it
> all works out the best, as I'll tell you privately also. She said to tell you
> also she will try to call down to the swamp with news sometime today
> if they know any more, as soon as that happens she'll call or ask some-
> one to, sometime today if they can get through, she means because of
> that phone.
>
> Duane

Good little note, and I just about memorized it the first time I
read it, but I folded it up, put it in my pocket, and carried it away
with me anyway, to show Roy.

It was a good sunny fall morning: chilly, but due to warm if the air
would stay in one place. The first thirty miles were paved, then I
turned off the highway and crossed the tracks and went east, and the
next seventy were dirt. Road was in good shape, good sandy road,
except for three short patches of clay—the longest one not a half-
mile—where you had to try to straddle the ruts. But I'm always glad
to see those clay ruts set like cement. Bad when it rains: even a half-
hour summer storm will make those clay spots so slick you can't
cross them. In the winter and early spring—late spring too sometimes—the road's closed.

So the men Johnny kept down there to fork hay to the cows
through the winter were out from under his observing eye.

But that never seemed to help Elwyn. He lived at the swamp with
his wife, and I doubt if he ever passed an hour without thinking a
thought about Johnny. Hated him with a passion.

On his side, Johnny didn't take Elwyn so serious as to hate him,
and I don't suppose he wasted a lot of time thinking about him, but
he hadn't much use for Elwyn, and he used to tell people so. Told everyone in the country that he only kept Elwyn on because if he fired

him he'd lose Roy (who was Elwyn's brother). Roy was the foreman, and one thing I'll say for Johnny, he knew what Roy was worth. Those tales got back to Elwyn. But the first thing he had against Johnny was Christine. When she was seventeen and Elwyn eighteen, and before either Johnny or Elwyn's wife Mary had been heard of, Elwyn had romanced the boss's daughter all one summer. Christine's father Mr. Tedlock got wind of it: found a bunch of drawings she'd made of Elwyn's face—probably made it look better than it did in real life, or just drew it a suspicious lot of times. Then he began noticing how her horse, which she'd ride all day every day, looked fat and fresh, considering; just the hobbles looked worn. Then he found some of her own hairs in the saddle blanket, and so he rode out himself and found the place up in the hills where they'd been sneaking off to. He plucked her up and sent her away to college—time for her to go anyhow. Worked fine. When she came back from the first vacation she didn't show much interest in Elwyn and avoided him—told him it was because of her father, and she may have thought so herself. Next time she came back she brought Johnny—and I'll bet after that the old man kicked himself for being so smart.

From the time I turned off the pavement I didn't see a soul or hardly a sign of one until I passed the sheep camp sixty miles in. Wooden trailer without windows, a loose-rock firepit that was still smoking, and a blanket and a shirt and a pair of wet socks hanging on a chokecherry bush. The man himself wasn't in sight. Down along the creek, I supposed, with his animals. Whoever employed him would have to be moving him and his sheep out pretty quick now if they didn't want to get them snowed on.

The Forest Service had laid a slab across the bottom of the creek. The creek was never dry and to lay that slab took some ingenuity (which isn't very typical of the Forest Service). I always meant to ask how it was done. In ten years it had never washed away, though plenty of acres had washed over it and sometimes pretty fast.

After you cross the creek you go up the other side and keep on another ten miles. The desert isn't flat but there's enough of a sameness to it, to the roll of it, so that you get lulled into thinking there's no end to it—especially when you've been driving along that far on a dirt road. So when you see that meadow under you all of a sudden and a bank dropping down to it with the road running at an angle down the side of the bank for half a mile, and you find your car on that incline, and a clay bank with a clay odor after all that sand, bunch grass, lava rock and juniper and sage—it's quite a fresh shock every time.

There're meadows sprinkled all over the desert up here. Most of them are smaller than the swamp, round as silver dollars—pretty little places up to a horse's belly in water in the spring. Called lakes: Grass Lake, Round Lake, Swan Lake, Smith's Lake. And since they have the names of lakes they make them blue on the maps, even fairly good maps; but I'd like one of those map-makers to have to get a drink from one of those blue lakes, say in August.

The swamp's round too, but so far across (about five miles) that you can't take in the roundness of it from most places. It's fenced, both around and down the middle, and in the summer half the meadow puts out enough grass to keep seven or eight hundred yearling steers, while from the rest of it they put up enough hay to keep a thousand cows through the winter. Which is what Elwyn and Roy occupy themselves at all winter: each morning they harness a team and sled hay to those cows. Takes four to six hours depending on the weather and the amount of snow on the ground. When there's no snow at all and you have to fight that mud is the worst.

The house was built in the only place it reasonably could be, where the bank levels off just above the meadow. Serviceable old house, though a ball would roll by itself on the floor of any room. Besides the house there's a barn, some sheds, a big set of peel-pole corrals, a little bunkhouse, a generator, a couple of privies, a couple of little milk-cow and calf pastures right by the house—just what you'd expect.

No smoke coming out of the kitchen chimney and I didn't see anyone around. I put my car in the shed by Roy's and carried my bedroll and satchel over to the bunkhouse and up the steps. I turned for a minute there on the porch before I went in. The big gate of the corral that opened out onto the meadow was braced open. Way across I saw what looked like a few people on horseback going out across the meadow.

I dropped my stuff on the first empty bed I saw; even this little bit of weight drove the springs down to the floor, which must have been why the bed was empty. I looked around: three of the six beds had bedrolls on them. One I recognized as Roy's. He lived in here the year around, though you couldn't tell it by looking. The others would be Gordon's and Shorty's—here for the fall cattle work like myself. I got used to the inside of the place after a minute and thought I remembered which bed I'd used last year. Empty, so I picked my stuff up and moved it over there. There was a note on it (Roy'd remembered my bed better than I had).

9:00

Murph—

    We are out making a short gather of yearlings from the middle field and will be in in time for dinner or sooner.

    Mary has gone along with us. She says for you to make yourself comfortable in the house, please.

    I'll leave old Roany trapped in.

Roy

Elwyn and Mary lived in the main house, and we all went over there for meals. I pulled out my watch: just ten.

I went to the house, made a fire in the stove, and drank some coffee left over in the pot from breakfast. No one around to tell my news to. Disappointed me. "Anyway, I'll ride out and meet them," I thought.

Roany's easy to catch anywhere if you take a bucket of grain— nice gentle little well-broke horse, but I was glad Roy'd closed him in the barnyard so I didn't have to walk out in the meadow through that wet grass. I tied him to a post over by my car (so I wouldn't have to carry the saddle), shed my coat, and brushed him down. Hair had thickened since I'd last seen him two weeks before—winter coming whether you like it or not. I saddled him and had the bridle in my hand when I heard someone start chopping wood.

"Must be Shorty," I thought. "Been pretending to sharpen his ax for the last hour or I'd have heard him before. Could tell him. Hardly worth trying to talk to though. Don't know how Roy puts up with it. What the hell, no one else to tell." Shorty's a little older than I am, worse off several other ways besides. Warrant out for him for one thing—which is why he likes to work way out here, though "likes" is the wrong word: old bastard doesn't appear to like anything. And deaf as a gourd, almost.

He saw me coming around the corner of the house toward the woodpile and sat down on the chopping block and leaned his ax up beside him. Don't know which he liked least, work or talk, but he wasn't about to do both at once.

When I was up about two feet from him I yelled: "Hi, Shorty, how are you?"

He spat, not in an unfriendly way but to the side, so that he could reorganize his tobacco and work his tongue. Only talked to about ten people a year and it got a little stiff.

"All right," he said. "How are you?"

"Just right!" I said. "Carrying news."

He pointed at his ear.

"News about Johnny," I yelled.

"Dead?"

That irritated me. "No, what makes you think he's dead?" I hollered.

He wouldn't answer.

"Sick," I said.

"Pretty sick?"

"You bet he is!" I said.

"You say he is pretty sick?"

"Damn your ears," I said to myself. "Yes," I yelled. "He's in the hospital."

"Huh!" he said.

I rode out. About eleven-thirty I came up to them. They were spread out behind a couple of hundred yearlings, bringing them in. Took me a while to make out which brother was which. Elwyn and

Roy look alike, even up close—small, slight men with small heads and delicate features, and fair. But when you get up close Elwyn looks a little fragiler, which he is. Roy's about forty-five, Elwyn a few years younger. Soon as I made out which one was Roy I angled that way; luck was with me and he was on the outside, so I didn't have to make it obvious. I came up alongside him; he stopped his horse and we shook hands, then rode along together behind the cattle.

"Made it down all right, Murph?" Roy said.

"Bearing news," I said. "Boss is in the hospital."

"Heck he is? What with?"

"Woke up in the middle of the night hurting and made Christine take him in—they don't know what it is, from the message I got." Elwyn, who was a couple of hundred yards off, raised his arm and waved. I waved back.

"Bear a lot of pain, too, can't he," Roy said. "Where was it hurting him?"

"Abdomen somewhere, what Duane says she told him, or what she told him to tell me."

"Must be then," Roy said. "Don't believe he has his appendix any more, showed me the scar once."

"They're going to run some tests on him this morning, have by now I imagine. Christine said she'd try to call down. Phone working?"

"Line's not dead, Murph. Crackles when you pick it up. Make out a voice at the other end half the time, other half you can't; sort of tell someone's there though. Damn that Johnny! Must have been hurting to let her take him to the hospital."

"Better than that, Roy," I said. *"Asked* her to take him. Look, got it here in writing." I took out the note and handed it over. Made his horse jump. "How'll Elwyn take it?"

"Agitate him," Roy said. "Bound to. Got to take the bad with the good though."

We put the yearlings in the corral. I rode over and shook hands with Elwyn, little delicate horny hand like a bird's foot; then with Gordon, great big fellow with big hands; and said hello to Mary, tall thin woman who only rarely let you know what she was thinking (and even that was too often). She hobbled her horse and went straight to the house to cook. We held the yearlings at one end of the biggest corral while Roy rode in among them and drove out several strays that had been down here all summer—all belonged to Sterling Green, another big rancher, and we let Sterling's back out on the meadow.

Then the four of us—Gordon, Elwyn, Roy, and me—led the five horses up to the barn, pulled off the saddles and bridles, put halters on the horses, and tied them to the manger, which ran all along one side of the barn, under the hayloft.

Elwyn climbed up a ladder into the loft and dropped hay down into the manger. When the hay fell in front of him Roany flung himself backward against my good halter and rope, sat down on his hocks, and started flopping back and forth on the line like a fish. Then the rope broke (if it hadn't his neck might have, but I was still sorry to ruin the rope), and Roany fell over backwards and rolled up against the wall, floundered there on his side, and then scrambled onto his feet again, making a devil of a lot of noise on that wood floor. When Elwyn heard the racket he peeked over the edge of the loft and called down: "Oh Roany, stop your clowning!" Roany stood there quaking, and shook his head and neck and twitched his ears like he wasn't sure they were still attached to his head.

I started looking around for another chunk of rope.

"Here, we'll fix it sometime, Murphy, take a fresh one," Roy said, and handed me another halter and rope. I put the halter on him and tied him up again. Gordon sat down on the edge of the manger and started to whittle a stick. The four other horses had held off eating to listen to Roany but they were at it now. Elwyn had come down; he stood behind Roany and patted him on the inside of the hind leg, then lifted his tail with one hand and picked some floor litter out of it with the other. Roany put his head down too, and started to eat hay.

"Okay, Roany, no more foolishness now," Elwyn said, "or we'll scrob your nob for you. You happen to bring any mail down with you, Murphy?"

"Brought it, it's in the car," I said.

"Look exciting?"

"Not hardly," I said; "couple of magazines though."

Roany had some splinters and smashed bits of meadow stems and shit stuck in the hair around his hocks. Elwyn started picking it out; horse didn't seem to mind and kept his head down eating. Last time I saw Elwyn calm for days. "Which magazines are they?" he said.

"Murphy says Johnny took to hurting in the night and made Christine take him up to the hospital," Roy said.

"In his belly," I said. "Might have it diagnosed by now. Christine said she'd try to call."

Elwyn's face looked like it was turned to glass. He didn't change his expression at all, or even move his mouth. "That so?" he said, and went on picking.

"I won't get my hopes up," Gordon said. "He's a hard son-of-a-bitch to kill, I'll say that for him, tried it enough times himself. She take him in by herself?"

"That's what I understand," I said.

"Must still have been able to lift himself around some," Gordon said. "Person doesn't want to get too elated. Reminds me; even if he dies, as I surely hope, person still won't want to get carried away. Old boy I used to know—worked as a foreman for another old boy who walked out behind a tree one day and shot himself dead—had more money than he could figure out how to spend or some other serious personal problem, I forget. Anyhow, with his boss dead this foreman felt such a load of weight lifted off of him that he went up-town and ordered himself a big steak—cut into his meat and the first bite he took his spirit had soared so high he forgot he had to chew and choked to death on the spot. Best not get carried away, that's the moral."

"I'll be up to the house," Elwyn said, and walked out.

"There's a man who can't stand to have his hopes raised," Gordon said.

Before we went in ourselves we stopped by the woodpile to get Shorty. "I told him about Johnny," I said to Roy.

"So Johnny's sick," Roy yelled at him.

"That's what I heard. What's he got?"

"Bad belly, Shorty, don't know," Roy said, and put his hand on his own belly.

We went in the house. "Elwyn tell you the news?" Roy said to Mary.

"Yes, I'm sorry to hear it," she said.

"Phone hasn't happened to ring since you've been in?"

"No," she said. Didn't seem in an agreeable mood.

I laid the mail down on a table by the couch. Elwyn was in the bedroom with the door closed. Roy'd started shuffling the mail and Mary'd just told us to sit down at the table when the phone started ringing shorts. Even Shorty looked over at it. Their ring was four shorts, and when it got to three we all stood still and waited, like you wait for the last cherry to roll up alongside the others on a slot machine—usually doesn't, and the fourth short didn't turn up either. I heard the bed creak. Poor man couldn't keep still, though he sure tried. Phone rang the three shorts a couple of more times and stopped. "Sounds like someone answered it," Roy said. After a few seconds he picked it up. "Barely hear them," he said, "but I think they're talking easy enough between themselves. Here, see what you make of it."

Gordon put his big ear to it. "I'd say they are talking normally, at a distance of about a million miles from here, if I had to guess."

"Fouled up between here and there then," Roy said. "Go ahead and hang it up. Well, that narrows it down to twenty miles of line. Two or three years we'll have it fixed."

Elwyn came out of the bedroom. "I'll be outside," he said, and walked out. Mary never said a word to him. Seemed to be spatting over his passionate attachment to Johnny. He never came in to dinner. Mary sat there like a wooden Indian all through the meal—ruined mine for me and probably everyone's but Shorty's. He kept his eyes on his plate (and his mouth almost on it too) and ate up.

Elwyn came in again while we were still at the table over coffee. Didn't say a word, but sat down on the couch with one of his magazines and pretended to look at it. Mary went into the bedroom and closed the door.

Minute later the phone rang four shorts. Elwyn wouldn't look up. "Damn thing," Roy said to the phone, and picked it up.

"Hello," he said. "Lo—" he yelled. "This is Roy Hill—damn near can't hear you—how's it on that side?—can you hear me?" "Man," he said to us, "think he said he can hear." "Hospital? That you Johnny? No? Driver?" He turned to us: "Who the hell's Driver?" "Hospital at nine? Don't get you. Cattle? Oh, cattle! Thought you said hospital. All right, think I got it. Just holler loud yes or no— you'll be here at nine in the morning after the cattle. . . . Good! They'll be here ready." And he hung up. Sweating like a horse.

"Hard of hearing, Roy?" Shorty said. Only joke I ever heard him make.

"Truck driver, Shorty."

Shorty nodded.

Poor Elwyn, he'd turned white and then he'd turned all colors. Left him kind of blue and he didn't look like he was breathing; still holding fast to his magazine. He got up on his feet for another march. Just then we heard the clack when she turned the key that shot the bolt that locked the bedroom door. He glanced in that direction, grabbed his hat, and went out.

We didn't see Elwyn all the rest of the day (don't know where he went—holed up somewhere, maybe up in the loft), and we didn't see Mary either. She told us the next day that the phone did ring late in the afternoon, and she said she answered it but couldn't make out a thing. I don't know if she really answered it. About a week later when I talked to Christine she said no one had.

There wasn't much left of the day. Shorty put in his time over by the woodpile, and Gordon and I stood around and watched Roy pull the shoes off a couple of colts he wasn't going to ride again till spring. We doctored a couple of bad-eyed yearlings, did the chores just before dark, and went back in the house for supper. Mary was in the bedroom and we got out of the house again quick as we easily could. From the bunkhouse we saw Elwyn cross the yard from the barn and go back in the house just a few minutes after we left it. Bet they spent a merry evening.

Roy built a fire in the bunkhouse stove. I looked through a couple

of old magazines, then walked over to the barn in the dark and
found my broken halter rope and brought it back and started splic-
ing it back together. Shorty lay on his back in his bunk chewing tobacco, and every few minutes he'd moan from the effort of gathering
himself to roll over on his side and spit (into a coffee can—he wasn't
dirty). Roy went to work braiding an eight-strand rawhide quirt that
he'd already half finished. Gordon took off his socks and went to
rubbing his big feet with bag balm.

About eight-thirty Roy put a big chunk of half-green wood on,
hoping it might burn most of the night. "Don't know whether to
turn the damper quite all the way down or not," he said.

"If you don't, nobody does," Gordon said. "You been building
fires in that stove for twenty years."

"Does she lock that bedroom door often, Roy?" I said.

"Hasn't for years, that I know of," Roy said. "Used to sometimes.
Surprised me to find out that bolt would still hit the slot; you know
how untrue all the uprights are in that old house."

"Sure," I said. "Boss may be back home by now."

"Likely," Roy said. "Wonder how Johnny is, Shorty?" he yelled.

"Sure thing," Shorty said.

"Stirs a person up," I said, and yawned. "Think I'll lie down."

"I'm going to in a minute too," Roy said, still messing with his
fire. "Gordon, you remember the day—must be fourteen, fifteen
years ago now, first summer Johnny came around—he tied a sack
full of cans to his saddle horn?"

"Sure," Gordon said.

"Hung halfway down the horse's leg, tow sack full of cans—little
invention of Johnny's for scaring the cattle with. Scared the horse
worse, and he naturally jumped about forty feet the first time the
cans jostled him, which was right when Johnny first tried to get on
him—he'd tied the sack on first. And Johnny fell back off but never
got his foot out of the stirrup, and the spur got twisted up with that
sack. Poor little scared horse running across that rocky desert and
trying to kick Johnny loose, what a sight that was."

"Battered him a little, didn't it," Gordon said. "Would have
killed him if the sack hadn't torn loose. Picked that sack himself out

of a whole pile; I remember thinking after it tore loose—'Whole pile of sacks and he'll pick the one rotten one.' "

"Hard on horses," I said.

"You couldn't scare him," Roy said.

Gordon had put the lid on his bag balm; he took off his pants and got in bed. "No, can't scare him—walk over a cliff just like a blind bull," he said. "I mean he would if he could walk."

"Remember the time he pulled the haystack down on himself?" Roy said.

"How was that, exactly?" I said, just to be polite. I'd heard it fifty times.

Roy fiddled with the damper one last time and got in bed. "Shorty—you asleep?" he yelled.

No answer.

"Shorty was there too. Well, we watched one of those professional hay haulers run up a big high stack of baled hay just like a monkey—hook in each hand right to the top. Had to be taking care to find toeholds and solid places in the bales to hook into—but you couldn't tell it. And naturally he couldn't pull too hard on any one hooking or it would pull loose and he'd fall off backwards. Johnny had to try it; and you know he clambered full speed up almost to the top, and plowed those hooks in so deep the hookings never pulled loose at all, but he leaned backward so hard he finally yanked some bales clean out and fell off backwards and those bales and that whole corner of the stack on top of him."

"Bullheaded streak even after he was crippled," I said. "I remember for a year Christine tried to get him to spend fifty cents for the cement for a little ramp for his wheelchair to go down from the kitchen into the garage—there used to be about a two-foot dropoff there. When he wanted to get to his pickup he'd leave his wheelchair in the kitchen and drag himself along the garage wall by hanging onto the cold-water pipes. Wasn't much trouble, strong as he is, and he wouldn't let anyone make him a ramp. And he'd go back from the pickup to the kitchen the same way. One day in there by himself at noon he slipped on the wet cement in that garage, lost hold of the pipes, and since they were up about five feet he couldn't get to them again once he was down. Christine had gone to town. He pulled himself along on the floor, but the kitchen door didn't have a regular knob for him to pull on and he couldn't get himself raised up high enough to unlatch the latch. Crawled back to his pickup then, but wore himself out so in the process that he couldn't pull himself back up in it either, and passed out on that forty-degree damp cement for two hours. Then at three o'clock he got up into his truck and called the sheriff, which is the only reason anyone ever found out about it."

"Quite a Johnny all right," Roy said, half asleep.

"Talk about him long enough and we'll start to wish him well," I said, and it crossed my mind right then that we were praising the dead, but there was so much wishful thinking in it I was ashamed to say anything.

"That would take more talking than I'm capable of," Gordon said.

"Don't think I'm good for that much either," Roy said.

"No, best go to sleep," I said.

About twenty to nine we heard the truck coming. "Truck's coming," Roy yelled to Shorty. We had the cattle ready to load and sat down on the loading-chute platform to wait. Driver would be coming straight from Klamath Falls, which wasn't our town, and Johnny'd be no more to him than a name on a hauling order, chances were, but he was the only hope we had and it wasn't impossible Christine had thought to send a message down by him, or more likely Johnny had thought to himself.

At the first sound of the truck Elwyn, who'd made a hand of himself all morning and helped us, though you could hardly get him to talk, disappeared again, walking off toward the barn with his head down. Afraid there might be news.

We heard the truck winding across the desert for twenty minutes before it came over the rim bigger than life and geared down the incline to the meadow. "Two people," Gordon said. Truck pulled right up to us, but with that high windshield and the morning sun coming from behind it we couldn't see who was in there until he opened the door on the passenger side and jumped out on the ground. Sterling

Green—old enemy of Johnny's from way back (though they'd never entirely quit talking).

"Tried to call you boys," he said; "thought we might just run those yearlings of mine in with the others, get them back up a little closer to home."

"We've got about three full loads, Sterling," Roy said, "but if there's room in the truck on the last load I don't suppose Johnny'd object—cheapen his hauling."

"Not likely to object all right," Sterling said. "I get my news out of the newspapers, but the way I understand it you boys have gone to work for a woman."

"Work for them in the long run anyway," Gordon said, "might as well do it directly."

"Johnny pretty well out of commission is he?" I said.

"Says so in yesterday's paper."

"Klamath Falls paper?—what time's that go to press—noon?" I said.

"Believe so, about then."

"Well, you're about as behind as we are then—though not quite. What's it say?"

"Here. I tore it out and put it in my pocket." And he pulled it out of his shirt pocket, little bitty piece of paper not even big enough to fold up. "Says he died of a sudden illness."

He held onto it while Roy and I looked. Gordon just glanced at it; Shorty sat over on the edge of the platform looking at us and swinging his legs.

"That's about all it says, too," I said.

"You wouldn't mind if I took that for a minute and showed it to Elwyn?" Roy said. "Might help him."

"All right," Sterling said, and handed it over. He hated to turn loose of it even for a minute.

"Dead!" Roy yelled to Shorty.

Shorty nodded.

Brotherly Love

There were five brothers in the family, but only two were close. And these two—Ben and Clyde— quarreled all their lives, from before they ran away from their parents' Colorado farm home together—Clyde was seventeen then, and Ben fifteen—until the end, when on his deathbed at fifty-five Ben was too weak to say anything more, though he probably felt like it.

Ben usually lost. At first he lost because Clyde was older and bigger and could knock him flat. When Ben caught up in growth, that time passed. And then, in their early twenties, as grown-up, sensible men, after one especially foolish and prolonged battle, the brothers swore off fighting with their fists.

But they still quarreled, and oddly enough Ben—who was the smarter and more articulate of the two—still lost.

Ben started the quarrels. Clyde didn't mind egging him on, but the truth was Clyde had lost interest and didn't much care whether he quarreled or not. And as a rule in brotherly quarrels, the one who cares more is generally felt by both to have lost, though the loser naturally never admits it. Clyde didn't care, so he won.

They quarreled over anything: horses and cows, women, games of chance, what time it was, work, promises, lies, a spool of thread Ben accused Clyde of borrowing and losing (until he found it in a drawer where he'd put it himself).

Since Clyde didn't start the arguments, it was over Clyde's supposed misdoings that they fought. Ben would have liked it if Clyde had tried—just let him try!—to take him to task. But Clyde, who worried very little over his own sins, didn't bother at all about Ben's.

Clyde was a self-satisfied man, and hard to get at. Poor Ben was left to stew in his own juices, losing one quarrel after another, until in the end . . . well, nothing happened in the end: they went on just like that until Clyde was left alone in the world without his favorite brother, a circumstance he quickly adapted to.

They did have some good arguments though, and once even came to blows again as grown men—an embarrassing thing to watch. Only one blow apiece was struck and no serious injury done: just a single cut, resulting in a scar which became more noticeable as Ben's hairline rose with the passing years.

Ben was just over forty when it happened—in 1945, during the war. For two years the brothers had been partners in a riding stables in Los Angeles. Business was good, and they were lining their pockets. They could hardly afford not to get along, and yet they had this big quarrel.

It's hard to say just when or where any particular quarrel between two such people begins. Ben's grudge against Clyde was continuous and seems to have begun when he himself began. Still, certain things happened.

Toni, who liked horses, came hanging around the stables, and Ben began to court her. Her husband was overseas, and Toni liked and encouraged Ben, who was twenty years older than she; and in his romancing he had some success—but never complete success. Faithful wife that she was, or was making up her mind to be, she made him suffer many fears and hopes.

Clyde had a good young horse. And when he offered to let Toni ride the horse, Ben's temperature rose. Ben said to her in Clyde's presence, restraining himself as much as he could: "He's a nice little horse, but I'm afraid he's livelier than what you're used to."

Clyde took the occasion to give her an unctuous compliment: "He's lively, but *she* can handle him."

Toni, who considered herself a pretty good rider, just smiled. She agreed with Clyde.

Whatever Clyde may have seen in Toni—and as Ben knew, he didn't loan his horses for the fun of it—Toni saw nothing in Clyde. And Ben in his better moments knew that, too. But she did want to ride the horse, a seal-brown gelding, and it would have been awkward to refuse. So she rode it, knowing she might cause a *little* trouble, but never dreaming how much.

In what followed, Toni was completely innocent—at least of intention. She fell off, or was thrown off—it was never decided, or rather, never agreed—knocked herself unconscious and couldn't remember for the life of her what happened. All she knew was that she was riding merrily along the canyon bottom, and then she was sitting alone in a ravine with a sore head and tears running down her cheeks.

At the very moment that this was happening to Toni, Ben and Clyde were up at the stables working away. Ben was taking money from a young couple who'd just signed the register (above which was a sign: RIDE AT YOUR OWN RISK), and Clyde was bridling the second of the two horses for the customers to ride. (Clyde and Ben had begun to make the customers pay in advance because some people—soldiers on leave were the worst—would ride the horses to the bus stop and abandon them. The horses would come back to the stables but the money, if you didn't already have it in your pocket, was gone forever.)

Ben was the first to hear the horse coming up the hillside and knew from the sound of brush scraping the saddle that the horse had got off the trail onto a deer trail and that no one was on it. "Dirty son of a bitch!" he said, as if customers weren't standing right in front of him.

The lathered horse rushed out from a clump of sumac, and Clyde slipped under the hitchrail and grabbed hold of the remaining rein (the horse had stepped on the other one and broken it off short). Happily, Toni's carcass wasn't dragging beneath, and the saddle was upright. But she could still have broken an arm, or even her neck. Ben got on one of the saddled rent horses and took off in a rush down the hill into the canyon.

He found her walking all in one piece along the canyon trail, got off the horse, and took her in his arms. Glad to see him, she laid her head on his shoulder—but only for a moment. Then she realized she had no great desire to be in anyone's arms. She was all sweaty and dirty and had a terrible throbbing head, and she was sure her eyes were red from crying. She wanted to go home. She was also embarrassed to have fallen or been thrown off and to have let the horse get away. "Is he all right?" she said.

"Sure, your horse is all right," said Ben, irritated, though not with her.

"He's not my horse," she said, and this made Ben feel better. He tried hard to think of something to say that wouldn't sound like "I told you so" but that would remind her that he had; but being a decent man he couldn't think of anything and kept quiet.

"Ooh, my head hurts," she said; "ooh," and she touched herself where it hurt.

"You've got quite a knot coming, all right," Ben said, examining it. She tried to pick some of the broken leaves out of her hair but it was impossible, they were so mashed in—right to the scalp. Toni felt little inclination to ride, but she'd never get home like this, so she took the reins and got up on the horse and Ben got on behind her, put his arm around her waist, and they rode back.

Clyde meanwhile, as soon as he'd sent the customers out on their horses, had unsaddled his own hot and frightened horse, thrown a light blanket on it, and led it around slowly (from the back of another horse) until it was cool.

Toni didn't feel up to facing Clyde just then. When she and Ben reached the top of the hill she rode straight to her car. Ben wanted to drive her home, but she said she could make it all right, and she promised to be back that evening. "I'm really sorry," she said. Ben told her there was no reason for her to be sorry and that he was just glad she hadn't been hurt worse than she was. "I'll go along with that," she said. She drove away.

She's a sweet girl, thought Ben. As he walked into the barnyard Clyde was running a soft stream of water out of the hose onto the horse's back.

"Took a spill," Clyde said. "How'd it happen?"

"Tossed her off," Ben said; "how'd you think?"

"That what she said?" Clyde asked.

"That's what the bump on her head said."

Later that afternoon, after the chores were done, Ben and Clyde,

without either one saying a word to the other about it, each rode
down into the canyon.

Ben went first. He followed the tracks, found the place it had happened, tied up his horse, and looked at the tracks and sign. In his
passion, it all seemed plain as day to Ben. The fool of a horse had
jumped (probably from some bogey of its own coltish imagination),
and instead of just shying in moderation like any horse, Clyde's
horse had jumped clear off the trail and over the bank into the
ditch—where it had begun to thrash and jump around in the deep-
piled sticks and leaves like a crazy thing, throwing Toni off.

He found the place where she'd hit. Ben squatted down and saw
where her head had struck in the cushion of old broken-up sycamore
leaves. He pulled a couple of long auburn hairs from this little nest.
All around were branches, heavy limbs, rocks. Had her head hit anywhere but just there. . . . And in dwelling on this stroke of luck, instead of his heart filling with joy he became angry. Why it might
have killed her!

When Clyde came along later in the evening, he read the tracks
and sign as carefully as Ben—and more coolly. She'd stopped the
horse in the trail and made him back up—just for the fun of it, because it's fun to make a well-trained, willing horse back up. That
would have been all right, if she'd watched what she was doing, but
the girl—no doubt not used to such a responsive horse—had backed
him right over the bank! And when the animal's hindquarters had
dropped down (the bank fell off about thirty-six inches), Toni had
simply tumbled off sideways.

And then the frightened little horse—wanting to get out of the
deep-piled sticks and leaves and away from the soft live body that
had suddenly appeared underfoot—had begun to jump and bound.
A less agile horse would have floundered right on top of her. But
Clyde's horse hadn't touched her, while she lay right there sleeping
like a baby, with a knot on her head. This was what Clyde saw and
figured out; and Clyde, dispassionate as a rock, was right, while Ben
in his frailty was wrong.

Clyde also saw the place where her head had hit, but unlike Ben
he didn't bother worrying about all the places it might have hit and
didn't.

Toni came back in the early evening as she said she would. Ben was sitting in the barnyard on the bench in front of the office, taking a rest, and Clyde's horse was tied to a post. She sat down beside Ben; he put his hand on her knee. Clyde appeared from the horse's stall, where he'd been breaking up a fresh bale of straw for bedding.

"Took a spill!" Clyde said to her. "That's too bad."

"I'm really sorry," Toni said. "I hope your horse is all right."

"Well, we all do it—the man who's never fell off one's never been on many. You take him out again if you want to." So said Clyde, but as a matter of fact he didn't like what had happened to his horse—and he took it as an omen and decided to leave the girl to Ben. But he thought he could at least be polite.

Toni got up and walked over to the horse. "Oh, his mouth's all skinned!" she said.

"He stepped on the reins some," Clyde said, "but it's a long ways from his heart. Don't think a thing about it." He didn't mention the rein he was going to have to patch, and which would never be the same again. He would have liked to say something good-natured about what it was like to ride a horse who backed up when you asked him to. But from delicacy of feeling he kept quiet.

"Well, thanks for the ride," she said, and laughed. "You too, donkey," and she reached and patted the horse on the shoulder: he started at the unexpected touch, and poor Toni jumped backward.

"Lots of juice in him yet," Clyde said.

Toni laughed without feeling like it.

Ben had kept quiet. It was typical of Clyde not to apologize for his fool of an overfed colt or for himself for letting her ride it and ignoring Ben's advice in the first place.

And even if Ben's construction of what happened was wrong, his indignation was just. It *had* been too much horse for her, as Clyde should have known, and she easily could have got her skull crushed.

There was plenty of seed for disagreement here, but the brothers in their wisdom wanted to get along. They had quarreled in the past, so many times, and where had it got them? Ben kept his mouth shut; and with less effort, so did Clyde.

Ben calmed himself with reasoning: Toni was unhurt. And as to riding the horse, she'd taken the cure. Clyde's behavior wasn't what it should have been, but there was nothing new in that. And after all, he, Ben, had been proven right, and that's always pleasant.

For all that, the thorn that was Clyde had been driven a little deeper into Ben's side.

Near the top of an infinitely long list of ways Clyde managed— without half trying—to irritate Ben was the way Clyde treated his horse. His very own horse!—as if it was any of Ben's business! And yet it was hard to put up with. Clyde kept the horse in a box stall, bedded up to its knees in straw (while shavings were good enough for the others); blanketed the horse at night; fed it grain three times a day (three times!—and not just plain old expensive oats, but a very fancy mixture of oats, bran mash, molasses, cod-liver oil, and all sorts of nonsense); Clyde brushed it, petted it.

But they might also have weathered this, which was after all a trivial business, and got along for maybe another whole year, and filled their sack with money, if one night Ben hadn't let the water barrels run over and flooded the barnyard. This put him in a bad mood, and then one thing led to another.

There were three of these wooden barrels on top of the hill, about a hundred yards above the barn and at the upper end of the big corral where the rent horses were kept. The pressure was low up there, and the barrels (which Ben had ingeniously linked together with hose, so that all three would fill from one setting) took about forty minutes to fill up—if it so happened that the day was warm and the horses had drunk the barrels almost dry.

The brothers had hired a man—Karl—who came up from the Soldiers' Home every day, or every weekday, to do this and that. He didn't do much and they didn't pay him much. He only had one leg and he was old. One of the chores they had given him to do was to fill these barrels. But it didn't work out. While the barrels were filling Karl wouldn't do a stroke of other work—just sat there. Besides, Ben found it an effort just to watch the old fellow limp up that hill, which he did with exquisite slowness.

So Ben had taken over the job himself. He'd do it in the evening, after the day's work was done and everyone was gone. (Clyde, who at this time had a wife—another reason the old devil shouldn't have been thinking of Toni—lived down in town, while Ben lived in the house at the stables.)

If he was in an easygoing mood and the weather was good, Ben would sit on the fence or even on the rim of a barrel, just sit and watch the horses eat their hay and quibble over it; whittle, day-dream, and think. Sometimes he became so contemplative that he could sit for long minutes just idly considering the barrel staves: if a barrel had been dry all afternoon the staves would have shrunk, leaving great cracks between them. You could pick them right up. And then when the water hit them they'd swell like sponges, until they pressed once again against each other and tight against the hoops.

But if he was nervous, or simply busy—if he was going out, for instance, and wanted to get ready—then he'd leave the water running, go over to his house, and come back later and shut it off.

And on this particular evening he was in no mood to sit still—far from it. He wasn't going out, though he *had* been. Toni had called. She'd received a letter from her husband in the afternoon mail, and she was in a state. She felt this and she felt that. He listened and tried to understand, and pretty well did understand—but so what? He'd still been stood up.

Ben might have comforted himself. If the past was any indication, this soul-searching of hers would only last three days and be much diminished on the third. And her husband, having no way of know-ing the service his letters did him, wrote infrequently. But just now Ben didn't feel like counting blessings of this kind. Shot out of the saddle by some jerk six thousand miles off!

He drove down to Art's Steak House in Santa Monica, ate some lamb chops, had several drinks and stared stupidly at two or three women, then came home and went to bed. At about three in the morning he sat up remembering the water.

Cursing, he pulled his pants, his socks, and his boots on—his socks weren't clean, making his boots hard to pull on—and cursing and cursing he went out and turned it off.

He saw in the morning what a puddle a dribble like that can

make, given a few hours. It had flowed down the hill to the nice level barnyard and there it had gathered: a regular little lake. And soon it would be no lake, with all the horse and human traffic there, but a mudhole. He frowned, thinking. If Toni came up, it wouldn't be so bad; he imagined the jokes he'd make on himself, and the way she'd kid him. But would Toni be coming? She probably wouldn't, and then again she might. If he only knew one way or the other, maybe he could stop thinking about it. But how could he know, when the woman's own mind was presently such a jumble?

Ben cursed away. When he tired of cursing out loud he muttered and cursed under his breath—but it would be a mire just the same. He took a shovel and started shoveling some little trenches, and to his satisfaction some of the water dribbled down them and over the bank.

Karl came limping up from the parking lot. The sight of the puddle tickled him. "I see I'm going to have to fire one of you brothers after all," he said.

Ben smiled as if cheerfully. "You'll have to give me my walking papers then, Karl," he said. "I'm the man."

Karl found the other shovel and began to help Ben.

Clyde came along five minutes later. (It was about seven in the morning.) "Looks like you boys are preparing to do some farming," he said.

"We'll plant tomorrow," Ben said.

The first thing Clyde did was to take down a halter from the peg and go get his horse from the stall. Every morning before he did anything else he brought the horse out, unblanketed him, and led him over to the trough to drink, which the horse usually did with great enthusiasm, plunging his face into the water—not just his mouth but his whole muzzle, nostrils and all, halfway to the eyes. He'd hold his breath and drink, swallowing hugely so that his Adam's apple rolled like a series of ping-pong balls throbbing along under the loose skin of his throat.

Today the puddle blocked the way to the trough—though there was no good reason why the horse couldn't walk through the puddle, or Clyde either.

Clyde—a cowboy to his very soul—was prejudiced against walking. When he did walk he didn't limp quite like Karl, but he hobbled along taking small steps in his size six high-heeled boots (he should have worn a six and a half, but he was too vain).

He by no means wanted to get these fine handmade boots of his wet (even though he had three pairs and these were the oldest). And anyway, he reasoned that it was the horse that was thirsty for water from the trough, not him.

But Clyde wasn't the only one who didn't want to step in the water.

Clyde brought the lively well-fed horse (overfed in Ben's opinion) out from the stall, led him to the center of the barnyard, unbuckled the blanket and pulled it off.

The soft canvas drawing across his back made Truth or Consequences wince. (He never called him by it, but this long and extravagant name was given the horse by Clyde himself.) Then he stood uncovered, slick as a fish; his coat, which was so brown it looked black, glistened, and with one eye he watched Clyde and with the other studied the puddle—an obstacle; he threw his ears forward and back, first one and then the other, like a semaphore.

Old Karl, who much liked to watch both the horse and Clyde's foolings with him, stopped and leaned on his shovel. Ben went on digging, though he may have watched from the corner of his eye.

Clyde ran his hand down the grooved back of the horse and patted his rump. The chaffy dust (full of expensive bran mash) flew up in little clouds, and the horse, who didn't like to be patted, picked up one hind leg and then the other nervously.

Clyde hung the halter rope over the horse's neck so it wouldn't drag in the mud, pointed the horse in the direction of the trough, urged him forward by giving a tug on the halter and clucking—and let him go.

The thirsty horse went forward—but didn't go so far as to even wet his dainty foot. At the very edge of the puddle he bent his neck down, sniffed the water, and whirled away. Clyde lunged for him and grabbed the halter, or Truth or Consequences would have been running around the barnyard, kicking up his heels.

"Get behind him once, would you?" Clyde said to Ben.

"He'll drink when he's thirsty," Ben said.

"He's thirsty," Clyde said.

"Not thirsty enough to drink," Ben said. But he got behind the horse and kicked sand at his hocks to frighten him while Clyde tried to keep him pointed in the right direction. No luck. The horse didn't want to walk in water; he jumped sideways and snorted. And as to kicking sand, he gave as good as he got.

"Lead him right up there," Ben said, "or else get a bucket."

Clyde didn't answer, but instead of leading or trying to lead the horse through the puddle or getting a bucket, he proceeded to double the lead rope over the horse's neck, making shift for reins, and clambered up on Truth or Consequences' back.

Clyde was short and had become a little pot-gutted—and he'd broken many bones, not all of which had healed as they should have—so he was some time getting even halfway up on the horse, who wouldn't stand still. Not that the horse quite dared to run off, but he kept wiggling and quivering and rolling his hide ticklishly, and he humped his back like an egg, right in the place where there's ordinarily a hollow, and where a person would like to sit.

While the horse performed in this way, Clyde couldn't get all the way up on him and didn't try to, but hung crossways over the horse's back on his own belly. In a husky unnatural voice brought about by his position (hanging with his head down and his diaphragm pressed against the horse's ribs) Clyde said: "Hog your back!"—which is what the horse was already doing.

Ben was afraid he'd be packing his brother off to the emergency ward as he'd done so many times before, but he didn't say anything. In response to Ben's thoughts, which Clyde was well aware of, Clyde, laughing and still hanging upside down and crossways, jabbed the horse in the foreribs with his knuckles. "Unhump!" he said. Truth or Consequences, like an unreleased spring that's been pushed from the side, didn't jump but humped still higher, sidestepped and shuddered and groaned as if ice were being poured over him. Then he subsided. Clyde, red-faced and with a sort of ungainly agility, scrambled up on him, petted his neck, and clapped him paternally on the hip again.

Then he took a rein in each hand, and with a little urging (Clyde pressed with his heels) the horse stepped into the puddle, gingerly at first; but as soon as his front feet had tried the mud and found it harmless, he walked forward, seeming to forget the man and everything, and eagerly put his head down into the trough and drank.

Then Clyde rode him back to the dry ground, but didn't get off. "I'll catch those rent horses and saddle them before long," he said to Ben. This meant that just now he wanted to go on riding his horse, and not to work, but that he didn't want to shirk his share of the work either.

Ben frowned. He wanted to get the horses saddled and ready early, so that he might sneak away downtown for an hour or two and do some "errands," though the only errand he had clearly in mind was to drive by Toni's.

"Plenty of time, isn't there?" Clyde said.

"I want to head downtown in about an hour," Ben said.

Clyde didn't ask why. "That's all right," he said. "When you feel like it, why just go on ahead. You work while I play, and then I'll do the same."

"I'm not going to play," said Ben grouchily. "I've some things to get."

"All right," Clyde said, "maybe you can pick up a couple of things for me."

"Just let me know what you want before I go," Ben said.

"All right." Ben was touchy today, Clyde saw. But that was all right too. He turned the horse. With his neck drawn up like a bow, the ticklish horse moved in tiny mincing steps up the hill to the gate of the ring.

Ben began rather sullenly to catch and saddle the rent horses.

From wherever he was—the rent-horse corral, the hitchrail, the raised porch of the tack room—it seemed he couldn't help seeing Clyde and his horse going round and round in the ring, cutting fancy little "sashays and didoes" (as Clyde called them) and figure eights and kicking up a lot of dust. Even when he couldn't see the man, he could see the dust.

Ben worked saddling horses while Clyde rode his horse; though pleased to consider himself a martyr, he at the same time took care to do no more than half the labor. There were nineteen horses to saddle, and Ben saddled nine and caught the tenth, led it down to the hitchrail and brushed it off.

Now he could go to town. But first he had to see what Clyde wanted him to get.

Ben walked slowly up the hill to the ring. He was tall and long-legged and walked with long, bent-kneed steps; on the way he couldn't help observing the remains of the man-made stream which had run down from the barrels, but he didn't now suffer any excess of feeling over this.

He walked up to the fence of the ring and waited for Clyde to ride over. Clyde, riding bareback with just the halter on Truth or Consequences' head, had loped his horse and walked him and now was loping again.

Ben hooked one of his skinny legs over the top rail of the low fence and leaned forward so that his knee touched his chest; he stood there, resting like this, looking like a standing crane or heron, birds he looked a little like anyway. (Ben was bothered by what he called a "nervous stomach," and in looking for relief from it he'd got in the habit of standing, sitting, and even riding in several peculiar positions.) Clyde, even if he'd wanted to, could not have stood as Ben was standing without being broken first and pressed. They were different, and yet there was a good deal of resemblance between the two: both were fair and had highly colored complexions (they turned red or white in the face easily), and they had high cheekbones, aquiline noses, and blue eyes. Ben's hair was red and Clyde's straw-colored, but they were both getting a little gray, and their wide-brimmed brown hats seemed to be a more legitimate part of their physiognomy than their hair.

Clyde rode over to the fence. The horse had a broad ruffle of sweated hair at the base of his neck and was puffing; his nostrils flared and subsided, flushed pink inside with the increase of blood.

"Feeling good!" Clyde said, and brought his palm down cheerfully on the rump of Truth or Consequences, who was too tired now and relaxed to quail.

"Uh-huh," said Ben. Ben stood there with his head turned just a fraction aside, as if his and Clyde's proximity were an accident and he didn't see why Clyde had picked this particular place to stop and rest his horse.

Ben acted badly—but he didn't think so. He thought himself sorely tried, as who wouldn't with a brother like Clyde. "I'm going downtown," he said. "You say you wanted some things?"

"Yeh I do," Clyde said.

"All right. What you want me to pick up?"

"Rivets and a couple of things all from the hardware—I'll make a list."

"I don't need a list. You tell me what you want."

They both knew what had happened not a week before: Ben had gone to town and forgot the very thing Clyde had asked him to be sure to get—a can of balm.

Clyde wisely didn't press it. If he had, Ben might have acted like a brute even sooner than he did. "All right," Clyde said, "I need a box of number four horseshoe nails and a sack of coal. I might tack some shoes on this little horse this evening."

"All right," Ben said.

"And some rivets," Clyde said. He still hadn't patched that rein.

Ben cursed himself for a silly fool to be so irritated by his fool of a brother. And right away, as soon as he was out of his sight in the big world, Ben felt better.

He went to a cafe and drank some coffee and, though it wasn't ten yet, ate a piece of pie. Freedom! He went to the hardware store and bought the shoeing nails, the coal, and the rivets, and then he did what he knew he shouldn't do—drove by Toni's.

But her car wasn't there. He was glad, because if it had been he knew he would have gone to the door—when she'd said outright that she needed to be alone. And where was it? Probably she was at Edith's—Edith's Dry Goods, where she worked parttime—unless she really was pulling something . . . and terrible thoughts, quite undeserved by her, went through his head.

He drove by the store, and yes, there was her car. He felt less ashamed to stop in at the store than at her house. Under the eye of

Edith not much could be said. It would be easy on Toni, and on him; and yet he could see what kind of a look was in her eye.

He was too superstitious to admit it, but he really expected to be reassured.

Expectation made the experience no less delicious. Her face lit up when he walked through the door.

And there was Edith—who allowed no hanky-panky at all, not in her store, or according to Toni anywhere else.

"Good morning, Mr. Webber," said Toni and held out her hand, which he was glad to shake.

"Hello, Mrs. Wilson, good to see you." They were old acquaintances!

He had to buy a pair of socks. He paid for them, and while the cash bell on the register jangled she formed clearly with her lips "I missed you."

She made out a receipt and he saw her write something across the bottom of it. He couldn't read anything unless it was held at arm's length, and then it wasn't easy. She knew that, but did she remember?

He took the receipt, twisted his neck, and wished, but the writing swam. She looked at him, perhaps expecting his face to express—what? He couldn't stand it. "I forgot my glasses," he said quietly.

"Oh," she said. "Well, you keep the receipt and look at it when you get home. I didn't cheat you too badly." She held out her hand once again, and he shook it. He folded the receipt and put it in his shirt pocket.

Back in his car Ben took out the receipt, unfolded it, and held it out and read what was written: "Bob Wills Tonight Only."

Ah, he knew what *that* meant. He'd heard the advertisement on the radio every morning for the past week until he was sick of it: "Remember—Bob Wills and his Texas Playboys, Wednesday, one night only at the Culver City Ballroom in Culver City. Don't miss it!" Well, she was hardly conveying this information idly! And "Tonight Only" meant . . . tonight! Well!

But Clyde was still Clyde, and when Ben went back to the stables, there he was.

Yet all might now have gone well, at least for that day, if there hadn't been a witness—of a particular sort—to the disagreement that took place that evening between the brothers.

It wasn't Karl—he'd gone home by then. If it had been him, or almost anyone but who it was—if it had been a stranger, for instance, or a prejudiced observer—Ben might never have worked himself to such a pitch.

As it was, Karl was gone, the customers were gone, and Clyde was just starting to shoe his horse, who'd never had shoes on before, when their old friend Jerry stopped by just to pass an idle couple of hours—he happened to be on this side of the city (Jerry also had an old trading horse in his truck that he thought he might be able to sell them for their rent string).

He'd known Clyde and Ben from way back, when they were all three just kids back in Rifle, Colorado, and ever since. Knew them, had heard them wrangle time and again, and wasn't much disturbed or at all titillated by these quarrels, but accepted them as part of everlasting nature.

Jerry had come along in the early evening; the stables were officially closed, the chores all but done.

Clyde had lugged out his anvil and set it near the hitchrail on its welded steel stand, had built a fire in the forge (out of sticks and paper), had added coal to the fire, and was now steadily turning the crank on the blower and heating the coal up red-hot.

Truth or Consequences was tied to the hitchrail—which was made of a two-inch pipe poured full of cement and strung through holes drilled in the tops of three big railroad ties that had been set four feet deep in the ground and in cement. And yet the heavy pipe was bent, from the pulling and lunging against it of horses, and the ties tilted toward the barnyard side—the side on which the horses were usually tied and where Truth or Consequences was tied now.

Ben and Jerry sat down on the raised porch of the tackroom (the edge of this porch nearly touched the end of the hitchrail). A half-dozen saddles lay there upside down, and some airing saddle blankets, still steaming, lay wet side up on the saddles. Jerry stood one of these saddles on end against the tack-room wall and leaned back against its sheepskin-lined underside.

Ben carried a straight-backed chair from the office up onto the porch, sat in it, and tilted it back against the wall, crossing his legs above the knee. If they hadn't wanted to include Clyde, they'd have sat over on the benches by the office where they usually did, in the shade, but that was too far away.

Clyde could have shod the horse in forty minutes, but it wouldn't be dark for more than two hours and he was in no hurry. Every time he came to a possible stopping point in his work, he stopped. And sometimes it seemed he would never start up again.

Right now, as soon as he had his fire going good and had stuck the two front shoes in to heat up—in other words before he'd really even started—he leaned against the pipe rail and began to jabber.

Truth or Consequences after his morning ride had been washed off and brushed down and had stood all the rest of the day in his stall and eaten a big feed of grain at noon besides. He felt rejuvenated. Everything enlivened him. At first there was the whir of the blower and the glow of the forge, the smell of coal and of hot metal; then there was the constraint of standing steady on three legs while the man held up the other; there was the smell of his own hooves burning when the hot shoes were pressed against them; the clang of the anvil; the unfamiliar *jar-jar-jar* when Clyde pounded the nails into his hooves. None of it hurt and he wasn't much frightened, but it certainly jangled his nerves, the more so as it went on—and standing still was hard.

But just now it wasn't so bad; he was standing at the rail watching the men, one leg cocked at rest.

"Isn't he a crackerjack?" Clyde said to Jerry. "You got anything like that in Gardena?"

"Sure I have," Jerry said. Being a horse trader he wouldn't deny it, but he was too lazy at the moment to lie extensively and to no purpose to Clyde, who he doubted was in a trading mood. Jerry sprawled out as close to flat on his back as he could without killing off the possibility of conversation. He blinked his eyes: the sun was getting low and trying to shine in his face—he pulled down his cap. Ben, for the same reason, tipped his hat forward and lowered his chin.

"You remember that old honcho of MacFarland's that I used to tie upside down in a ditch to shoe?" Clyde said.

"Uh-huh, I do," said Ben patiently.

"No one else would touch her. Used to pay me fifteen dollars and glad to get it done."

Ben felt the paper crinkle in his shirt pocket every time he moved. "I'll be back directly," he said. He had a phone call to make. He went into the office, closed the door, and called. All was well. She said she'd drive up to the stables around eight-thirty.

"Where's Miss California Sweetheart this afternoon?" asked Jerry.

"She'll be around after a bit," said Ben, and winked.

Ben and Jerry walked down to Jerry's truck and spent twenty minutes looking over the horse, which they both knew Ben wouldn't buy. Ben climbed up and sat on top of the racks, looking down, and Jerry got down inside and petted the horse, tugged on its tail, and pried open its mouth so Ben could see inside.

With nobody around to talk to or to listen to him, Clyde worked. He held up each hoof and shaped it with knife and rasp and made it level. Then he took a hot shoe out of the forge fire and held the shoe against the flat bottom of a front foot for measure. Then, before the shoe had a chance to cool and harden, he took it to the anvil and pounded it into shape to fit the hoof.

Truth or Consequences could hardly take it all in. The hot shoe sizzled noisily against his hoof and the strong-smelling smoke poured off as if he was burning alive. The anvil clanged; the shaped shoe hissed when Clyde plunged it into a bucket of water.

Clyde put a lineup of horseshoe nails in his mouth, picked up the same front foot, held it between his knees, and began nailing on the first shoe.

Each time the hammer struck, the horse gave a little tug with his leg, as if to see whether Clyde was ready to give the foot back yet so that he could place it back on the ground, which he would very much like to do. Innocent and halfhearted as these tugs were, they were enough to rock Clyde backward and to break the rhythm of his hammering. He had to pause, to search for his balance, to dig his feet into the uneven ground again—and it was very annoying. "Give it here," he'd say to the horse, "I'll hit you in the belly with a rasp, you pea-brained son of a bitch." But he wasn't about to hit the nervous horse in the belly, for it would have caused him more trouble than anything.

With his head under the horse's belly and almost touching it, Clyde hunched over, his feet splayed out and his knees knocked together, the horse's leg between his knees—and sometimes it felt as if he was holding up the whole horse. Whatever he said (mostly he swore) sounded breathless and sibilant: breathless because he was standing all scrunched up, and sibilant because he had those horseshoe nails between his teeth and had to curse without opening or entirely closing his mouth.

It was hard work, putting on even this one shoe. He nailed the shoe to the hoof with seven nails; he drove the nails at an angle, toward the outside, and as each nail came through he twisted off the sharp end with the claws of his hammer; then, by holding a small steel block against each protruding stub and giving the head of the nail another blow or two with the hammer, he bent the stubs back tight against the hoof; then he clinched the nails down even tighter with the clincher and smoothed off the whole row of clinches with the smooth side of the rasp. At last Clyde stood up, gave Truth or Consequences back the foot with a parting curse, and wiped his sweat-bathed brow. Ha! It was hard work, and no one pays you to shoe your own horse. He leaned against the rail, resting one hip on it. Ben and Jerry were back, and had taken up their old positions.

"Looks like brother exercised himself a little after all," Jerry said. "He'll get that colt shod before dark if he's not careful."

"If I don't it won't be the first," Clyde said. "We've shod more than one old skate by lantern light, huh Ben?"

"Sure have," said Ben agreeably.

"Ben—" Ben looked at him— "you remember that little bay mare belonged to old what's-his-name out there on the Madeline Plains by Ash Valley? What was his name? —Little old bay mare had swirls and whirls all over her like a guinea pig: Curly, he called her. Can't remember the man's name. She'd curl you one right in the eye, too, you didn't watch her."

"Dunlap," Ben said.

"Dunlap," Clyde said, "you're right! I remember one time I—"
And he described how he'd shod Curly through the expedient of ty-
ing her hind foot to her tail; and then without breaking stride he
changed the subject (more or less), and while the sweat dried all over
his body and the horse got more and more antsy, Clyde, who liked
standing still just fine, turned around and planted his back against
the rail, took hold of the pipe with both hands as if he wasn't ever
going to let go, and while he was describing in some detail the way in
which in one long day he'd shod *nine* horses, five of them so wild he
had to tie them down flat on their backs to get shoes nailed on their
feet, his own horse turned sideways of the rail, backed toward him,
laid back his ears, and began to rock forward and back like a hobby-
horse, lifting both hind legs off the ground each time he tipped forward, as if threatening to kick.

Ben, who at first was a little amused by this, began to be made
nervous as it went on. The horse appeared to be lifting his hind end a
shade higher at each stroke, and Clyde made no move. Ben couldn't
take his eyes off the horse and could hardly listen to what Clyde was
saying (which in itself was no great loss, since Ben knew it all by
heart).

"The last one was a mule," Clyde said. "It was damned near dark
and I'd had all the bending over I wanted. So I said to the old boy
that owned him: 'How about this mule? Is he about as gentle as
these other broncos of yours?' "

"If you're going to go on talking, you better move over on the
other side of that rail," Ben said.

"What for?" Clyde said. He glanced at his horse. "He's just playing. 'He might be a gentle mule,' the man said, 'I don't know anyone
who's ever got close enough to find out.' So I—"

"He'll play hell with your knee when he kicks it, too," Ben said.

"Nah—he don't mean anything by it," Clyde said. "So I said, 'I'm
a little tired of bending over. You ever see a mule shod upside down
in a ditch? It's a lot easier to reach their feet.' And this old boy says:
'No, and I don't want to.' "

"I imagine you talked him into it," Jerry said.

"I did. I told the man, 'Well—' "

But Ben was beside himself and wouldn't let his brother talk. "I guess he didn't mean anything by it when he threw Toni on her head—just playing?"

Poor Clyde could only take so much, and this time he answered Ben back: "He didn't throw her on her head any more than he's fixing to kick me right now. She banked him—I mean backed him, off a bank and fell off him. Not that I hold it against her."

"Is that right?" said Ben nastily.

"Yessir, that's right."

"You don't hold it against her?"

"No, sir."

"He came that far from killing her,"—Ben held his thumb and first finger up with no space whatever between them—"and you don't hold it against her?"

Clyde chose not to repeat himself and was silent.

Ben's lips compressed into a line. Jerry looked at them both and mentally shrugged.

Truth or Consequences was still bobbing up and down. "Lookit here, Jerry," Clyde said, and he picked up the rasp, put it in its scabbard—in order to make a louder noise—and clapped it against his leather shoeing leggings.

At the sound the horse jumped sideways away from Clyde, hit the end of the halter rope lightly (so as not to hurt his neck), drew up short and stood, nervously and attentively flicking his ears as if to say "What next?"

Ben turned red in the face and looked down at his hands.

"Ain't he a crackerjack?" Clyde said.

"Nice little horse all right," said Jerry politely.

Jerry took three cigars from his shirt pocket and offered one to Ben, who took it but didn't light it and finally put it in his pocket; one to Clyde, who took it and walked over and lit it in the forge fire and began to smoke, coming back from the forge to exactly the same place at the rail to do it; and Jerry lit one himself. He sprawled back, puffed on his cigar, and wished the brothers weren't so edgy with one another.

The horse turned toward Clyde and began the same bunny-rabbit motion as before. This time, irritated now and excited, he went on like a good one, lifting his feet higher and higher and then adding the trick of throwing out his hooves so that his hind feet snapped in the air and made a sound like a towel being snapped; and they came closer and closer to Clyde.

Tight-lipped and coloring more deeply all the time, till he looked like a brick, Ben watched. There was a small pop as an unshod hind hoof slapped against the frayed end of Clyde's legging, just below the knee. Jerry blinked. Ben remained expressionless. Clyde glanced down at himself and kicked dirt at Truth or Consequences, who jumped away from him and turned the other way by the rail and began to kick higher and higher and more boisterously into the air, finally clanging a foot against the pipe, after which he stood still; he held his bruised foot up and shook it, switching his tail grouchily.

Ben got up, and averting his face picked up a saddle, carried it into the tack room, and flung it violently onto its rack. Jerry shook his head.

Clyde nodded toward the horse and said to Jerry: "He'll scratch your back if you ask him to."

Jerry watched the horse shake his bruised foot. At least there was plenty going on to occupy his attention while he sat and smoked, and the sun had gone down behind the office and wasn't in his eyes any more.

"He might scratch it where it don't itch," he said.

Imagine Jerry's surprise when Ben without a word sprang past him from the door of the tack room, down the steps and straight at his brother and struck at him with his long powerful arm almost before Clyde could straighten up from the rail.

But either Ben's heart wasn't in it (which is hard to believe), or Clyde shifted his jaw enough to make the blow a glancing one.

Clyde swung the rasp, which luckily for them all was not only in its sheath but came down on the crown of Ben's hat, which absorbed a little of the blow. But there was plenty left over to deliver the message, and Ben fell forward on his face—scaring the wits out of the horse, who flung himself backward so hard that the rope broke.

Scared as he was, the horse was the first to calm down, and he

spent the next twenty minutes—during which he was free to do just
as he pleased—nosing around the haystack pulling a little out of this
bale and a little out of that (as if it wasn't all the same).

Clyde dropped the rasp in the dirt, and he and Jerry crouched over
Ben, afraid to touch him. "Let's turn him over," Jerry said.

Clyde put his hand on Ben's shoulder. Ben groaned and began to
put his hands under him: he wanted to get up on his hands and
knees.

They lifted him under his arms, and with his knees giving way he
half walked, half was carried over to the bench in front of the office,
where they sat him down. Blood was running down his face.
"Where's my hat?" he said.

"Right here," Jerry said, "but you keep it off. You boys have any
bandages around here?"

Ben shook his head. "I'll fix up something," Clyde said. "You
mop his face off. Here." He gave Jerry a handkerchief and pointed to
the faucet.

Clyde went up to Ben's house, managed to find a couple of clean
undershirts, folded one into a compress and ripped the other. Once
bandaged, Ben put his hat on, but it wouldn't fit down over his forehead and he had to tilt it back like a movie star.

"How you feel?" Clyde said.

"Little woozy. My fault," Ben said and extended his hand, which
Clyde shook gently.

"Don't think a thing about it," Clyde said. "We better take you
down and get a few stitches in that. I'd do it myself if I had a good
needle."

"Here comes a car," Jerry said.

"That'll be Toni," Ben said.

It was almost dark, and she looked at Ben and then took another
look. "What happened?"

The three men were embarrassed. "I rode a horse into a tree,"
Ben said.

This weak tale was far from satisfying Toni; but she kept quiet till
they were alone.

Ben happened to look at the broken chunk of rope dangling from
the hitchrail. "You put your horse up?" he asked Clyde.

"No—by golly!—I better go find him."

After a few minutes Ben stood up and found himself steady on his feet. It was decided that Clyde and Jerry might as well go their ways, and Toni would take him to the emergency ward.

"Now you boys behave yourselves," Jerry said, and drove away in his truck.

"Goodnight," Ben said to Clyde; "sorry we didn't get that colt shod."

" 'ats all right," Clyde said gruffly—and held out his hand to Ben. They never shook hands, and now they'd done it twice in twenty minutes. Then Clyde turned and walked off.

"What really happened?" asked Toni as soon as they were alone in the car.

"I hit Clyde and he whacked me a good one."

"You *hit* him? Why did you do that?"

"Just seemed like he needed hitting."

"But what did he do?"

So Ben tried to explain what Clyde had done. But it sounded to Toni—and even to Ben—as if Clyde hadn't done much of anything.

They were lucky that it was a Wednesday night: the emergency ward was running slow for business. After getting fifteen stitches sewed into his scalp they went on to the dance, where Ben had a few drinks and soon felt no pain.

Ben's mood—not only tonight but for several days—was one of calm exhilaration. All the animosity had been knocked out of him. He felt as if there'd been a devil in that head of his, who'd flown out.

But Clyde felt bad. Less than anyone did he understand why Ben had hit him. Like a bolt out of the blue. Why? Didn't like the way he went about shoeing his horse? Made no sense. Afterward, Ben was sorry. But why had he done it? If the man had done it once (which he certainly had), then he might do it again. And be sorry again—if he was still able. Who knew what shape one of them might not end up in?

But they weren't married. The next morning Clyde didn't show up for work, and he didn't come in the afternoon, either. Ben called: Clyde wasn't home, and he had only told his wife that if Ben called to "tell him everything's all right," and she seemed honestly to know no more about it than that.

The following day a letter came, or rather an envelope with a note in it: Clyde never wrote a letter in his life.

August 15, 1945

In good faith I, Clyde Webber, hereby sign over my half interest
in the B-19 Ranch Riding Stables to my brother Ben Webber.

Clyde Webber

The old devil had even had it stamped and signed by a notary.

Ben drove straight to Clyde's house. But Clyde was his old self,
and it was impossible to get anything out of him.

"What's this?" Ben said, holding up the paper.

"I've got a bottle of Jack Daniels here," Clyde said. "Want a hit?
Sit down."

"Thanks, not today," Ben said, and touched his forehead. They
both laughed. "Now what's this business?" He held up the note.

"Man can't do the same thing all his life," Clyde said. "I took a
job."

"A job?—what job?"

"Troubleshooter in a steel mill."

"What for?"

"Pays good. Person gets tired of doing the same thing every day."

"Seems to me it came a little close on my popping you one."

"Happened to, but they been trying to get me to take this job for
some time."

"That right? Well, if that's what you're going to do, I'm going to
pay you for these horses and saddles and all—there's ninety ton of
hay there all paid for, you know—half yours."

"No you aren't," Clyde said. "I don't want it."

Ben wrote out a check—but there was no way to make Clyde cash
it.

For two years after this Ben behaved himself pretty well toward
Clyde. They didn't see each other regularly, and didn't work together, so it was easier than it might have been.

Then for a year Ben didn't see him at all. Ben had saved six thousand dollars and leased a ranch up in the Mother Lode country. After Ben had been there a year, Clyde came to visit. And it was ap-

parent, from what Clyde saw more than from what Ben said, that Ben was losing money hand over fist. Clyde asked Ben to take him on as a partner. Ben procrastinated, and privately he grumbled, but in the end he agreed.

Clyde saved Ben's skin, but with the two once again at close quarters, a fat lot of gratitude he got in return.